The Long Road Home

LORI WICK

HARVEST HOUSE PUBLISHERS
Eugene, Oregon 97402

All Scripture quotations in this book are taken from the King James Version of the Bible.

Except for certain well-established place names, all names of persons and places mentioned in this novel are fictional.

Cover by Terry Dugan Design, Minneapolis, Minnesota

THE LONG ROAD HOME

Copyright © 1990 by Harvest House Publishers
Eugene, Oregon 97402

Library of Congress Cataloging-in-Publication Data

Wick, Lori.
    The long road home / by Lori Wick.
    Sequel to: A song for Silas.
    ISBN 1-56507-590-0
    I.Title.
  PS3573.I237L6   1991
  813'.54—dc20   90-20607
                                                                 CIP

To my own
sweet Abigail,
precious gift of God.
I'm so glad He knew I wanted you.

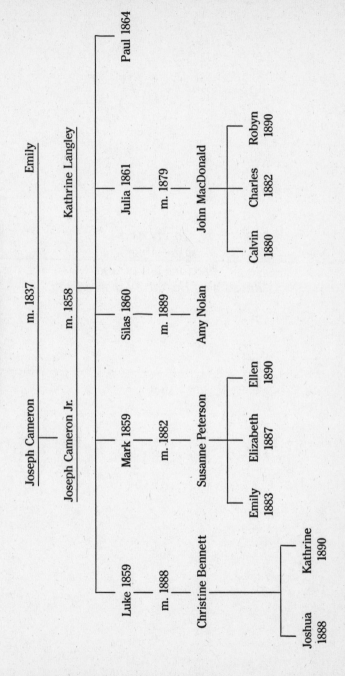

CAMERON FAMILY TREE — 1890

FOREWORD

Neillsville, Wisconsin
October 1889

Seated side by side in the wagon, Silas and Paul Cameron headed to town. Though neither one knew when he would see the other again, the ride was strangely silent—or maybe it was because of that fact.

Paul knew his life would be changing radically in the next few months. Bayfield—his destination—was no quick trip home to Baxter. Baxter...having just been there, Paul wondered when he would see his family again. He said a quick prayer of thanks for being able to stop off in Neillsville where Silas was staying. Otherwise he wouldn't have seen him at all before going to his new job.

A bit of excitement shot through him at the thought of going up north. He had already spent a few weeks up there preaching and talking with the congregation, and then waiting for their decision When they called him to be their pastor, he accepted, knowing that it was not a matter to be taken lightly. He had committed himself to preaching every Sunday, and there was no predicting which days he would be called upon during the week. As he finished up his visit with Silas, Paul was glad that they had given him permission to delay his start with them. Once in the pulpit, there was no foreseeing when he would be this way again.

"I wonder what's going on. Everyone seems excited about something." Silas' voice cut through Paul's thoughts and caused him to look around. The citizens of Neillsville did seem to be in a dither over something.

"Hmmm, I don't know."

They continued on to the station. Once there they both noticed the relative quiet of the train yard after the din of town. They spoke to no one, but comments came to them as they waited—something about a mob at the banker's home because the bank had been robbing people.

Paul and Silas exchanged looks a few times but said nothing. When Paul asked Silas if he wanted to go now and check into the situation, Silas declined. "I'll go after your train leaves. Maybe things will be calmed down enough by then so I can find something out."

Paul's arms went around his older brother, and the men embraced as the train vibrated to a stop. "Take care of yourself, Paul, and write. I'd like to meet Corrine."

"You'll meet her. As much as I'll miss all of you, I can't wait to see her again." Silas laughed with understanding as the two men embraced.

Paul boarded the train and waved to Silas from the window. He then stowed his bag and settled into his seat. Within seconds his mind was on the woman waiting at the end of his journey, and he smiled.

Corrine Maria Templeton. Tall and very slim, she always seemed unbelievably fragile to him. Her skin was clear and pale, accenting her blue eyes—eyes that always held just a hint of pain, Paul thought. He wished she were beside him, and then smiled at the impatient thought. They couldn't be together soon enough for him. He'd felt that way since the first Sunday he had preached in Bayfield and met Corrine at her aunt and uncle's.

Just a few weeks ago Paul would have laughed at the idea of love at first sight, but something had happened that day, there was no denying that. He was sure of what he was feeling, and once in Bayfield he would only have to see Corrine to know if he had mistaken the look in her eyes.

As the train increased in speed, Paul's mind moved briefly to his finances. His grandmother had given him money for the train fare to Bayfield, and he had been very thankful.

"Maybe," he thought to himself, "I should have told her how little money I have." Almost as soon as the thought entered Paul's mind, he dismissed it. He had enough to get where he was going. Once in town he had a home with Corrine's uncle and aunt, Lloyd and May Templeton. They would take no money for his room and board, so Paul really had no pressing financial needs. He was especially thankful for not having to take work outside the church like so many pastors of small congregations.

The trip was a long one, and Paul changed trains more than once. Paul's bag held his Bible and, when he wasn't dozing or visiting with some of the other train passengers, he read. The train moved rapidly past scenery that was breathtakingly beautiful: rolling hills and valleys, grassy areas with little more than a few flowers, or dense areas of forest where trees, towering far into the sky, cast long shadows over the land.

By the time the train rolled into Bayfield, Paul's long legs felt cramped. He was glad the Templetons lived uphill from the depot; he needed the exercise.

As he walked a sense of well-being overcame him, and he praised God from the depths of his soul. This was his town now. God would use him to reach out to this bay-side village and show them the way to Jesus Christ. He pictured Corrine by his side and felt as though God had placed the world at his feet.

"Oh yes," Paul thought, as he walked up the steps of the home in which he lived, "Corrine and I are going to win Bayfield for God."

1

Bayfield, Wisconsin

A few weeks later Paul sat thinking on his sermon of that morning. It had gone well. The congregation had been warm and receptive. He felt he was off to a fine beginning in his new church.

But soon his thoughts turned elsewhere and he grew anxious. Where was she? He began to whistle tunelessly and bounce his heel on the floor in quick rhythm. His eyes caught those of his hostess, and he quickly stopped.

Paul's stillness lasted only seconds before he had to restrain himself from pacing the floor of the elegant front parlor. The Templetons, aware and greatly amused over the young pastor's plight as they sat across from him, wisely kept still. They knew that as soon as their niece arrived, the anxious look on his face would disappear, to be replaced by a look of rapt attention for Corrine alone.

Amid Paul's impatient vigil, the front door opened and in walked the love of his life. He was vaguely disappointed to see she was followed by her parents. He had somehow hoped she would come alone. But just looking at her as she crossed the room to take a chair near him banished all other thoughts from his mind.

Paul looked at her closely as she took her seat. He knew she had been in poor health lately. Paul had known great frustration at not seeing more of her, sure that he could be a comfort. She was pale but as lovely as ever in his eyes. Paul's attention then turned to watch her father, Hugh Templeton, settle his weight in a delicate chair and look about the room in his usual disagreeable fashion. Paul wished he could march right over to the man and tell him of the love he bore for Corrine and ask for her hand in marriage.

But Hugh Templeton was an unapproachable man, and his expression was constantly stern. Paul learned in a hurry that if Hugh hadn't liked something about the sermon on any given Sunday, he wasted no time in telling Paul. Paul also realized, on the other hand, that if Hugh enjoyed the sermon, he said not a word.

Attempting to talk to Corrine beneath the scowling regard of her father was more than Paul could take, and he despaired of being able to say two words to her.

He finally gathered courage and leaned forward, intending to tell Corrine how pretty she looked in her gown of pale yellow, when Mr. Templeton's voice broke through rudely.

"Well, Corrine nearly dragged us from the house to come here. As if I have nothing better to do with my Sunday evening than sit around May's fancy parlor."

His tone and words were lost on Paul as he watched Corrine blush becomingly, telling him how much she had wanted to come. Paul and Corrine would have sat for unknown hours and stared at one another if Corrine's uncle had not broken in.

"Corrie, why don't you and Paul head out and ask Matty for something to drink?" Lloyd could feel his older brother scowling, but he ignored him.

He believed Paul Cameron to be a fine young man and, unlike his brother, didn't believe Corrine, as sweet as she was, to be too good for *any* man.

The two young people nearly stumbled in their haste to exit the room. Paul reached for Corrine's hand the second they were out of view and didn't release it until they entered the kitchen at the back of the house.

Corrine greeted her aunt's part-time cook, Matty, and told her of their request for refreshments. Matty was old, but not so old that she would mistake a couple in love. She told the young people in her stern way, "I can't possibly take a tray into that parlor without some fresh flowers sitting on it. Now you two get outside and bring me what you find in bloom."

Grinning like fools, they turned without a word and raced to do her bidding. "And don't you rush the job, either," she called after them. "If I don't like what you pick, I'll send you right back out."

They ran down the back steps like small children running from a mischievous act. Paul waited only until they were out of view before he pulled Corrine into his arms and kissed her for the first time.

Paul broke the kiss to find Corrine blushing furiously. She moved away from him and began to pull wildflowers from a small patch. Paul knelt beside her, and they worked for a time in silence. The last time they were together they had had so much to say, sharing from their hearts all their hopes and dreams, but now—Paul wondered if he should apologize for kissing her.

"I'm sorry, Corrine, if I was presumptuous just now, but the truth is, I missed you very much and thought about you the whole time I was away."

They were standing now, and Corrine turned to face Paul, her expression tender with love. "I missed you too," she admitted quietly.

Paul needed no further encouragement, and in the next instant Corrine was back in his embrace. "Marry me, Corrine," Paul said and heard her gasp. "Oh Paul," was all she was able to say before he kissed her again.

"I love you, Corrine," Paul said finally, thrilled beyond reason at being able to tell her.

"And I love you, Paul Cameron," Corrine stated simply. Their hearts overflowed with joy, unable to believe they could ever be happier. The flowers were forgotten as they held hands and made plans.

"I'll talk with your father and we'll be married right away." Paul's voice was breathless with excitement, and Corrine clung to him for a final embrace. They walked back to the house, the flowers they had picked left on the ground, both completely unaware of anything but each other.

The next days flew by in a flurry of anticipation and nerves as Paul tried to gain courage to approach Corrine's father. He saw Mr. Templeton more than once, but each time Paul's fear of the man overcame him, and he said nothing.

He was busy with his work at the church and had to fight resentment at being called upon to do his job at times when he wanted to be with Corrine. He knew without a doubt that his feelings were wrong, but at times he was unable to control himself.

Paul spent more time in the Word and prayed for strength. He still believed God wanted him and Corrine together, but it would have to be His timing and not Paul's. When Paul settled into this mind-set, his entire outlook changed, and a wonderful peace settled over him as he was used of God in his small church.

The church had not had a full-time pastor in years, and Paul rose to the challenge to see his small congregation reach their full potential. Paul spent extra hours on his sermon and spoke to two women about singing solos.

He even baby-sat one afternoon for a few hours when a young mother took sick. Paul gained a new appreciation, as he and his four- and five-year-old charges walked all over town, for the job a mother has in raising young children. Paul believed the joy of a pastor was far more than standing in the pulpit on Sunday. It was also getting involved with the people and becoming a part of their lives, so for him it was all part of the joy and another opportunity to serve God.

And always at the back of Paul's mind was Corrine and the life they would have together, and praise to God for giving them each other. But as victorious as Paul had been over his willfulness and the joy he was experiencing in his work, he was not prepared for the confrontation with Mr. Templeton the next Sunday after church.

When he saw Corrine and her mother making their way to their buggy and Mr. Templeton hanging back, he assumed he was going to hear how bad his sermon had been. Paul had him figured out now. The man did not like to hear that all men were sinners and needed Christ. This fact surprised Paul because he knew Corrine and her mother to be believers. It made him wonder why Mr. Templeton continued to attend.

The last of the congregation had descended the steps, and Mr. Templeton stood before him. Paul was taller than the man, but Hugh still intimidated him to the point that he felt like a small boy in trouble. Knowing the Scriptures he was going to use this time, he waited patiently for the man to speak.

"Corrine has never been as robust as her older sisters." Paul stared incredulously at the man, wondering what in the world he could be talking about.

"She's not sick, mind you," Mr. Templeton hastened to add. "Just not as strong as some girls—never has been. Now I think you're an alright man for a preacher, but you're not for my Corrine.

"She's young yet, and when the time comes that I think she should find a man, well, it'll have to be one who can keep her in the fine things she's been used to all her life. There's no reason for you to take this personally, but I'm her father and I know what's best." Without another word, Mr. Templeton turned and walked away.

2

If there was anything worse than being kept from the woman you love, Paul couldn't imagine what it could be. Corrine was in the same miserable state as Paul and looked so down the first few Sundays after Paul had been warned off that he feared Mr. Templeton had told her some awful lie about his not wanting to see her.

But his fear didn't last long as he saw Mrs. Templeton, seemingly standing against her husband in that she made sure Corrine stayed in line to shake the pastor's hand, as was the custom of their small congregation.

It was during those times that Paul was able to tell Corrine by the touch of his hand and the look in his eyes that none of his feelings had changed.

Paul continued to pray, seeking God's guidance in this painful matter of the heart. Still confident he and Corrine were to be together, he was sure of it after Corrine had missed two Sundays in a row and a note arrived, asking him to come to the house.

Paul had never been asked to the Templeton home before, and he was a bundle of nerves as he approached the large, two-story home. When he walked in, Corrine was waiting in the living room, with a woman Paul didn't recognize.

If Paul thought her pale and slim before, he was unsure what to think when he saw her this time. There were dark circles beneath her lovely eyes, and her dress hung loose as though she'd had a sudden weight loss.

Corrine had obviously been very ill, and Paul felt rage at not having been called to see her. With little regard for the third person in the room, Paul walked directly to the sofa, sat down, and reached for Corrine's hand. Joy leapt in the young woman's eyes, and Paul realized she had been unsure of his reaction to her.

His heart nearly broke over the fact that she had doubted his love, and his arms were around her in the next instant pulling her to him. The act was too much for Corrine, and she began to cry. Paul said nothing as he held this dear woman, her body so pathetically frail, but his resolve was strengthened. This was right. She belonged here in his arms and, as soon as he could, he would speak to her father.

Corrine was gaining control of herself and she shifted to move from Paul's arms, but they only tightened around her.

"I won't let go of you, Corrine," She tipped her head back and looked into his face, and he went on.

"You belong here in my arms, and I'll not be ordered from your life again. Nothing has changed. I still love you and want you for my wife. Your aunt said you were under the weather, but had I known how sick you were, nothing would have kept me away."

"Oh, Paul, I've missed you so. I prayed every day you would come, but I knew in my heart you would respect my father's wishes and stay away. He doesn't understand, Paul, that you are the man I've prayed for all my life."

Her words made Paul's heart soar. He said nothing but just drew her close, holding her tenderly and thanking God for allowing them to be together as well as asking for strength to speak with Mr. Templeton.

Paul didn't have long to wait. The Templetons entered a few minutes later to find Paul and Corrine embracing on the sofa. When Paul became aware of their presence, he released Corrine but stayed seated and took her hand.

"Mr. Templeton, Corrine and I want to be married. I love her and she loves me. I promise to cherish her all the days of our lives, and I'm asking for your blessing."

Some emotion, unreadable and fleeting, passed over Hugh Templeton's face. Then his eyes shifted to his wife who had taken a seat and sat with her hands clenched tightly in her lap. Paul thought a brief look of regret passed over his features as he then looked to his daughter.

"Is this really what you want, Corrine?"

Paul felt her head move near his shoulder in the affirmative and watched Mr. Templeton nod. He gave them no time
to thank him but turned and walked from the room. Paul
thought he looked like a man defeated and right then
resolved to make him never regret that Paul Cameron was
his son-in-law. God would give him and Corrine a good life,
of that he was sure. They may not have many possessions,
but Paul knew God would bless them and take care of them.

Corrine was still weak, and Paul found out what a woman
of strength her mother was. She included Paul in every
stage of the wedding plans, surprising and pleasing him
when she told him how soon the wedding was to be. Immediately couldn't be soon enough for Paul, so no one heard
complaints from him.

Corrine was still not up to full strength as the day neared,
and Paul was becoming concerned. He questioned her, and
she told him it was a recurring illness she'd had since
childhood. She said it wasn't unusual to go for months
without a trace of pain, and then other times it seemed to
come and stay on for a while.

Paul could see as she answered him that she was becoming anxious about him changing his mind, so he dropped
the subject but prayed daily for God's healing of the woman
he loved. As he looked ahead on the days to come, even
with Corrine sick, he knew he had never been happier. God
was using him and now he was to have a wife by his side as
he worked. Corrine had a heart for the people of Bayfield—
he'd found that out the first time he had met her. Paul knew
that together they could do anything God asked of them.

If Paul felt a little worried about Corrine's illness, the
moments were brief. God would heal her and use the two of
them for His glory.

3

Two days before the wedding, Corrine was completely bedridden. Paul begged her to change the wedding date, but she was adamant. He stood by her bed in acute frustration. The woman Paul had first seen in the living room and found out later was Corrine's nurse was seated quietly nearby.

"Corrine, you don't even have the strength to get out of this bed. I don't mind waiting until you can be up."

It was no use. Corrine had made up her mind, and Paul couldn't change it. What surprised him the most was that her parents were all for them being married immediately.

"We were thinking, Paul," Mrs. Templeton spoke to him in the hallway outside her daughter's room, "we can hold the ceremony right in Corrine's room. I know it's not what you planned, but it would make Corrine so happy, and she's had so little happiness."

Paul wondered at that statement, even as he heard himself agreeing to the plan. Why, to hear Mr. Templeton talk, Corrine had had the best of everything her entire life.

Paul and Corrine were married two days later. Corrine's nurse had helped her sit up against the headboard, and Paul stood next to the bed, her hand in his.

As pale and sick as Corrine looked that day, hope surged through Paul. He knew this was the beginning of a wonderful marriage. He thought of the children they would raise together and praised God with all his heart for His goodness and love. If he had to spend his wedding night in the room next to Corrine's and not with her, it was a small thing really in the light of all the years they would share.

The days that followed developed into a pattern of sorts. Paul took all his meals at his wife's bedside, and the entire house seemed to brighten as their laughter was heard again and again.

They shared with each other from the deepest recesses of their hearts: their hopes, dreams, plans, and prayers. Part of their daily routine was a time of prayer for their life together as man and wife. Even when Corrine's health continued to decline, Paul did not despair. God had great plans for them.

Lunch time was their favorite time to discuss plans for the future.

"Do you like blue?"

"Umm hmm," Paul answered around a bite of fried chicken.

"That's good, because I'd love to have a blue kitchen. I dream about having a quilting bee around my own kitchen table in my own blue kitchen." Her voice was so wistful; Paul prayed silently he would be able to give her that wish very soon.

"How many ladies from our church attend the quilting bee?"

"I think three, but the entire group is probably 15."

They ate for a few minutes in silence. There was potato salad to go with the chicken and baked beans. Paul's favorite pie was for dessert, and he had just taken a bite when Corrine asked about his Sunday sermon.

"I'm in the last chapters in Genesis, and I think it's going fine."

"I wish I could be there."

"Why, Corrine, what's the matter with me? We always have prayer, but it never once occurred to me to have Bible study together."

"Oh Paul, could we really? I so miss your preaching. You're a wonderful pastor—the best I've ever heard."

Paul leaned over his wife's bed and they shared a loving kiss. "We'll start tomorrow, and I apologize for not thinking of it before." Paul's word was good and they did begin the next day. Corrine had wonderful insights to the passages they studied, and Paul found himself learning from her.

They still prayed every day, and often Paul felt tears in his eyes as he listened to his wife pray for the people of Bayfield. She had grown up here, and her heart was committed to seeing the people she'd known for years understand that Christ died for the sin of all men.

When Corrine's condition worsened to the point that she could no longer feed herself, a doctor was sent for. Paul did not look at this as a sign of defeat, but of hope. Surely God would use this man to heal his wife.

But it was not to be. Corrine's condition deteriorated with each passing day. Her room was now a constant swarm of people: Corrine's parents, the doctor, and three nurses for around-the-clock needs. Paul often could not even approach the bed. When he could get near, it was only to stand at the foot and watch his wife's pale face on the pillow.

Still he trusted in God. Stories of Jesus healing the blind and lame, Scripture passages of Jesus walking on the water or calming the sea came constantly to Paul's mind. His was a God of miracles, and Paul knew the healing of Corrine Cameron was going to be one of those miracles.

The days passed slowly. Corrine was not aware of anything now—not of her nurse straightening her pillow or of her husband who stood for sometimes hours and watched her sleep as her breathing became lighter, shallower with each passing hour.

Paul left her side only for brief times. He wanted to be the first person she saw when she again opened her eyes. Finally, in exhaustion, Paul retired to his room to fall fully clothed onto the bed for a time of fitful sleep.

He awoke some hours later to a commotion in the hall. Rising from the bed disheveled and disoriented, he stumbled to his wife's room just as the doctor was turning from the bed. The doctor looked to Corrine's parents and gently shook his head. Paul watched Corrine's mother bury her face in a handkerchief and felt as though he were in a dream.

For the first time in weeks Corrine's room seemed to be clear. Paul approached the bed, still not believing the evidence staring him in the face. His wife could *not* be dead He had prayed; he had asked God to heal her. She could *not* be dead.

Paul looked down at his wife's still form. He stared at the sheets over her chest for a long time, but there was no movement. For days her breathing had grown quieter, barely audible, and now there was complete silence.

Paul reached out and picked up her hand. Lifeless. In that instant, something cold squeezed around Paul's heart. What a fool he had been to think she would live. Her parents had known, he realized now. His prayers, his belief had been useless. They had encouraged the wedding because they knew she was going to die. He wondered if Corrine had really known how serious her condition was.

God had let her die. God had done this. Paul bent over his wife's body. Her brow was cool as he gently kissed her. His eyes moved over her beloved features one more time as his hand smoothed her hair. He looked at no one as he turned from the bed, and no one spoke to him or tried to stop him. It didn't take him long to pack his few things. After all, he didn't possess much—he was just a poor preacher.

He thought absently as he left the house in the still dark of night that he really ought to let his grandmother know there had been a change in his plans.

4

Bruce Mines, Ontario

Even as Paul dealt with the loss of Corrine, another family, many miles away in a Canadian province, was also saying good-bye to a loved one.

"The Lord gave, and the Lord hath taken away; blessed be the name of the Lord." The minister's final words were spoken through clenched teeth, necessary to avoid chattering. The frigid wind whipped at coats and skirts, causing the handful of mourners to huddle even deeper beneath whatever covering they wore. The service was over, collars were pulled higher, and movements were stiff as the people began to walk away from the grave.

The two grave diggers stood off to one side. Even in gloves, their hands and fingers felt like ice as they gripped the handles of their shovels. They watched until the only mourner left was a small woman. Seemingly unaffected by the wind and cold, she wore a coat that was threadbare in places. She stood looking into the hole, and the men could see her mouth moving, although the wind didn't allow them to catch the words. Assuming she was praying, they looked away to give her privacy.

The woman had not heard anything anyone had said to her, so deeply was she drawn into her grief. Now, if anyone had really cared to observe, they would have realized she was not praying but speaking into the grave.

She didn't begin to pray until she turned from the hole in the ground and then only to plead, "Please, Father, help me."

Once out of the cemetery and into the churchyard, she made straight for a wagon. The older man and woman standing beside it watched her in opposite fashions. The woman's eyes were filled with sorrow, compassion, and love, while the man's eyes were cold and angry. He spoke as the young woman neared.

"It's all your fault he's dead. You and your religion, you and your work for God. There was nothing wrong with his life the way it was, and then you come along and fill his head with 'life for God' talk." The words were spat at her in anger and bitterness. She stood in agony and let them come. "I can't stand the sight of you! He's dead and you're alive. I wish you were dead, too. You get your things and get out of my house."

Both women watched the man stomp away, leaving them with the wagon and horse. The older of the women spoke when her husband was out of earshot. "He's wrong; he's so wrong." The woman continued even though tears clogged her throat. "He's out of his head with grief, and I'm not sure he knows what he's saying, but he *is* wrong." The woman reached and hugged the younger woman.

"I could never have asked for a more precious daughter-in-law, and I know my son had never been happier before he met you and turned his life over to God. But you do have to go away. I'm afraid for you if you stay here because he's so angry and bitter." They were holding on to each other's hands now, and the older woman's voice became desperate. "Are you listening to me?"

The younger woman nodded, pain squeezing her heart at the thought of leaving this woman whom she loved, this woman who was the mother of her husband, now the only tie to his memory.

"You must go away for a time. I've got a small amount of money, enough to see you out of town and I'm not sure how far. Maybe you could go spend some time with your aunt in Wisconsin."

They looked at one another and hugged again, each one unable to see any other road to take at this point. They climbed aboard the wagon and went back to the house to pack a bag for the young widow.

At the house, the grieving father did not make an appearance. After packing her few belongings, she was able to get to the train without mishap. It was just as she boarded, took a seat, and looked out the window back at the train station that she caught sight of her father-in-law. He stared at her—his face still a cold mask of bitterness.

Again she prayed the only words that would form in her grief-soaked mind: "Please, Father, help me."

5

Paul stood quietly in his grandmother's living room, his back to two of his brothers—Luke and Silas—and his brother-in-law, John "Mac" Mac-Donald. Emily Cameron sat just in the next room at the kitchen table, petitioning God with all her soul on behalf of her youngest grandchild.

Without turning, Paul spoke. "I came here to tell Gram of my plans, not get a sermon from my brothers."

"I thought giving sermons was your job," Luke said.

"Not anymore." His voice was implacable, hard.

"Paul, I realize I don't know how you feel, but I don't believe for a minute that God has deserted you. I—"

"That's right, Silas. You don't know how I feel, so don't say God hasn't deserted me. How was Amy when you left the house today, Silas? She was fine, wasn't she? Don't forget for a second you still have a wife and haven't the faintest idea of what it feels like to bury one."

Silas had no reply to this, and he exchanged a look with his brother and Mac—they just as helpless as he in the face of Paul's bitterness.

"Your sister will want to see you, Paul." Mac spoke now, his deep voice gentle. "I don't know what I'll tell her if you go without seeing her."

If the men could have seen their brother's face, they would have known Mac's words had hit home. Paul and Julia had always been close. But Paul took a moment and effectively pushed his sister's face from his mind.

"Just tell her I'm sorry I missed her."

"I'll tell her, Paul, and I'll tell you outright. I'm disappointed in you. I've never known you to be so selfish."

24

Paul turned from the window at this remark, his voice cool. "I don't agree with you, Mac, considering I wouldn't have seen any of you if you hadn't been here working on Gram's house. I can hardly be sorry if my plans don't include a visit to everyone."

"What about the plans for your church? What will the people in your church do for a pastor?"

Paul turned once again to the window upon Luke's question. It wasn't his problem any longer. He couldn't possibly go on teaching about a God he could no longer trust.

He had trusted God at one time—trusted Him with everything. But God had let him down. When he believed God could take care of the most important person in his life—Corrine—God had failed him.

Anger and bitterness surged through him, and it was evident in his voice, a voice his brothers knew better than to argue with. "I'm leaving tomorrow, and all the talk in the world isn't going to stop me. I'm not sure where I'll end up, but I told Gram I would stay in touch with her."

Grandma Em sat in the kitchen and listened to the words and then the sound of someone going up the stairs. She had never felt so totally helpless.

It didn't take long for the three men remaining downstairs to move into the kitchen.

Luke asked, "You heard?"

Grandma Em could only nod.

"I'm afraid he's going to have to work this out for himself." Mac's voice was sad and resigned.

"He's so bitter." Grandma Em's voice was filled with anxiety. "I would have thought nothing could make Paul turn his back on God."

"I feel the same way, Gram," Mac assured her. "But regardless of Paul's feelings, God has not turned *His* back on Paul. He's still God's child and, no matter how far down Paul goes, God will be faithful."

"We never even met Corrine." Grandma Em sounded as if she had just realized this. The table fell silent, each person experiencing grief over the loss of a granddaughter/sister-in-law he or she had never even seen.

Upstairs sat the man with whom they grieved, even more bitter than they imagined, making plans to walk down a road that would take him far from his family and into a life where his God would not be welcome.

6

The train into Baxter slowed and then came to a complete stop. Abigail Finlayson sat and stared out at the small station. This was the end of her journey, but she couldn't bring herself to move. Her wish as she had begun the journey from Canada was that she could just open her eyes and be there, but now that she had finally arrived, she was terrified.

From her correspondence with her Aunt Maggie, Abby knew her aunt worked for Dr. Mark Cameron and lived with his family. She felt tears coming on over not knowing if she could even stay with her aunt. If Maggie lived in someone's home, then she wouldn't be at liberty to have her niece stay. Abby felt herself on the edge of panic. In her state of exhaustion, she couldn't think clearly.

Abby stood with her hand tightly gripping the seat. On legs feeling as if they were made of wood, she moved to the door. A man was there to help her step down. She thought she detected a look of pity, and instantly knew she looked as bad as she felt.

Her eyes felt as though they had sand in them every time she blinked, and a quick hand to her hair told her it was hanging in limp strands.

Abby moved stiffly toward a man standing by the station door. "Excuse me, sir. Can you give me directions to Dr. Mark Cameron's home?"

"Hey, Mac," the man suddenly shouted without answering her question, making her start in surprise. "This little gal here is looking for Mark's place. You got a minute to take her by on your way home?"

Abby was horrified at having gained the attention of everyone within shouting distance. When a man of tremendous size moved toward her, she was sure she would have run if she didn't think her legs would betray her.

The first man moved on, shouting something to one of the men on the train, and Abby was left to face this "Goliath" on her own. Why, with her diminutive height, the top of her head barely reached his chest pocket. The man named Mac spoke the minute her eyes met his.

"I'm headed past Mark's right now. My wagon is parked over here." These words said, he stepped aside and waited for Abby to precede him. Abby knew she was staring rudely, but if the big man noticed he gave no indication.

Abby's legs trembled as she walked toward the only vehicle parked in the direction he had pointed. He probably eats small redheads for breakfast, Abby thought. Her normally fearless personality was crumbling at her feet in the presence of this man of such intimidating size. She would have been embarrassed to tears if she could have seen the smile on Mac's face.

The walk to the wagon was almost more than Abby could bear after the many hours on the train with very little to eat and almost no sleep. She was unaware of the way Mac had stayed behind her as they walked, intending to help her into the seat. So when Abby stopped by the wheel and swayed a bit, things suddenly getting fuzzy, Mac's hand was instantly there to steady her.

"It's a good thing we're going to Mark's."

"I'm not sick," Abby said faintly. For a moment the giant's face swam before her eyes. "I'm looking for my aunt, Margaret Pearson."

A smile stretched across Mac's face. "Maggie's niece! She didn't tell us you were coming."

"She doesn't know."

"Well, that won't matter. She'll be delighted to see you."

Abby didn't share his confidence. She was feeling worse by the minute and wished she had gone home to Michigan, even though there was a slight chance her father-in-law would look for her and that would be the first place he would check. Abby shivered slightly as Ian Finlayson Sr.'s bitter features sprang up in her mind without warning.

Mac lifted her gently into the seat and watched her carefully on the way to Mark's. He was sure she was not even aware of him. Maybe it was her small size, but she reminded him of a homeless red kitten. He couldn't remember ever seeing anyone with red hair and gray eyes before. He was sure that on a better day she would be quite lovely, but for now the pale features—lips absolutely bloodless—were a bit frightening to him. He was sure he would be taking her to Mark's even if she hadn't asked.

7

It took a few seconds for Abby to realize the wagon had stopped moving. The seat beneath her shifted, and then Mac was standing ready to help her over the wheel.

"My bag! I left my bag on the train!"

Compassion filled Mac's heart as he reached beneath the seat and pulled out Abby's small case. She hadn't even remembered his taking it before they left the train station.

She stared stupidly at it for a moment, wondering how he could have produced it so quickly. But before she could gather her thoughts, he spoke. "This is Mark's house. Let's get you down and inside where I'm sure we'll find Maggie."

They were halfway to the front door when it was opened by Susanne Cameron, Mark's wife. Sue naturally assumed upon seeing the bedraggled, pale-looking woman with her brother-in-law, Mac, that she was a patient.

Mac would have walked directly into the house but Abby, desperately trying to get her bearings, stopped on the front porch.

"I'm sorry to intrude on your home like this," she began, hoping she was addressing the lady of the house. "But I'm looking for Margaret Pearson. Is she here?"

"Abigail!"

Abby's head snapped up at the calling of her name to see her aunt standing beyond the blonde woman in front of her. Abby didn't notice Mac slipping past her or he and the woman moving out of earshot. Her eyes were locked with the concerned ones of Maggie.

"Abby?" Maggie's voice was questioning as she moved to the door.

"Aunt Maggie," Abby spoke quickly to get the words out while she could, "Ian is dead. I had nowhere to go. His

30

father blames me, and he's so angry I was afraid to go home. I'm sorry I couldn't write you, but I..."

Abby stopped talking as Maggie reached out and drew her into the sturdy circle of her embrace. She clung to her aunt, this woman who was so dear to her, but even then she didn't cry. Not one tear had she shed since the news came to her that her husband was dead.

Maggie simply held her niece gently and let her mind focus on the spat of rushed words that had poured from her. Ian Finlayson was dead. Maggie suddenly couldn't remember when they had been married, but she knew it wasn't long ago. Even as questions swirled through her mind, the nurse in her came to the fore.

She pulled gently away and held Abby at arm's length. Abby looked awful. Her usual peaches-and-cream complexion was washed out to nearly a shade of gray, and her beautiful hair was slick with oil and perspiration. Maggie was sure she had never seen so much pain in such young, lovely eyes.

Maggie led her niece through a house Abby took no notice of, to a small, neatly furnished bedroom.

"Is this your room?" Abby had enough presence of mind left to realize she was sitting on someone's bed and her aunt was removing her shoes.

"It's my room and my bed and you're going to get into it." Maggie's voice was more brisk than usual to cover her concern for Abby.

"It's time for bed?"

"It is for you," Maggie answered her, thinking Abby sounded like a lost little child.

"But where will you sleep?"

"Probably right next to you." This time Abby noticed the extra briskness.

"Are you angry with me, Aunt Maggie?"

Maggie turned away from the window where she had moved to pull the curtains closed. Her voice softened slightly, but she knew her niece and knew that too much softness right now would be the worst thing for her.

"I *will* be angry if you don't get right into that bed. You're probably hungry, but I think you need sleep more." Her next words were from one nurse to another. "Do you want some laudanum to help you sleep?" Maggie nodded at the slight negative shake of Abby's head and began to dig in the small traveling bag in hopes that her niece had packed some sort of night garment.

Maggie was just tucking the covers in around Abby when there was a knock at the door. She opened it to find her employer standing outside.

"Sue tells me Mac brought your niece here from the train station. Is there anything she needs?" He had moved toward the bed as he spoke and was now looking down on the half-asleep young woman in Maggie's bed.

"Aunt Maggie?" Abby called for her, a bit fearful of this tall man by the bed. He looked kind, but she was sure this was the doctor, and she *had* come completely uninvited into his home.

"This is my niece Abigail Finlayson, Doctor Cameron. Abby, this is Doctor Cameron. He wants to make sure you're alright."

"Do you want me to leave?" Abby asked the man, unaware of the way her voice trembled.

"No, I was just thinking that after you've rested a while, you should move upstairs. We've a room we use for patients who need to stay over."

His words were enough to bring Abigail to full attention, making her usual determined personality cloud over her good sense. She tried to get out of the bed even as she spoke. "I'm not sick and I'm not a patient. I had no right moving into your home in this way, and if you give me a few minutes to pack my things..."

Mark did not touch her but sidestepped to block her flight from the bed and waited until she looked at him. It was a mistake on Abby's part to tip her head back because the room began to spin. She mumbled, "I'm not sick," even as she felt hands tucking her back beneath the covers.

Mark was thinking that if he wasn't so worried about her he would laugh. She was Margaret Pearson's niece alright. Levelheaded, determined, strong, and nobody's fool—until she got physically down in some way. He knew the young woman before him was a nurse just like her aunt, and nurses made the worst patients—almost as bad as doctors.

Abby told herself to get out of the bed and talk to the doctor. She was not sick, just tired and hungry, but her body would not obey the commands of her mind. Voices came to her as she fought off the exhaustion flooding over her.

"Maggie, why don't you take the upstairs bedroom?"

"No. I want to stay close to Abby. We've shared a bed before, and we'll be fine tonight."

"Maybe that's for the best. She appears to be as poor a patient as you are."

"I don't know what you're talking about," Maggie said with an indignant sniff. "I never get sick."

Had Mark not been very conscious of the sick woman in the room they were exiting, he would have laughed outright on that statement.

8

Abby bent over the large oak bed to smooth the last of the wrinkles out of the quilt. As she straightened, an image of her and Ian snuggling in bed came to mind, and she turned away in an effort to dispel the sight.

The downstairs was quiet, and Abby wondered where Mrs. Cameron could be. She found coffee on the stove but made no move to help herself. She had been living with Mrs. Emily Cameron for nearly a week, and she still felt awkward and strange. It wasn't because of Mrs. Cameron, of that she was sure. It was just that since she had awakened in Dr. Cameron's house, really woke up and realized where she was and that Ian was gone forever, nothing had felt or seemed right.

She had met nearly all of the doctor's family on Sunday after church and they were all very kind, but they didn't fill the void, the hollow feeling that seemed to invade her when she least expected it.

Thankfully, the church service had not lasted too long. It had felt like something akin to torture to sit there and listen to the preaching, sound as it was, and know that Ian would never preach again.

Ian's image appeared as he had always looked in the pulpit: serious, sincere, and strong in the Word of God. Abby was able to push that thought away, but another one replaced it. It was the one that had haunted her for the past 17 days since his death. The look she saw on Ian's face this time was the one he'd had when Abby had explained new life in Christ and Ian had understood. What an awesome thing it had been to be used of God in this way—to help someone understand that in God there was a better life because of the life His Son gave for all men.

Again Ian's face was before her and it was serene and filled with a peaceful joy. She tried to push the look aside before her heart burst with pain and loss, but it wouldn't go and Abby knew why. It was because of the promise.

"Good morning, Abby. Sorry to run out on you like that, but the day was so clear and fresh-smelling I got side-tracked in the garden."

Abby smiled slightly at her hostess' enthusiasm but said nothing. It was much warmer here than in Canada, she thought absently. The freezing wind at Ian's funeral came to mind, so when the older woman began breakfast Abby pitched in to help expel her morbid thoughts.

"Mrs. Cameron?" Abby said, intending to ask her a question about setting the table.

"Abby, everyone calls me Grandma Em. I really wish you would." When Abby didn't answer, Grandma Em went on. "It won't work, you know. I can tell you from experience that what you're doing won't work."

At Abby's confused look and continued silence, Grandma Em went on. "You see, Abby, grief and I are old friends. And right now you're sure if you never let yourself get close to anyone again then you'll never be hurt again. It won't work. Believe me, I know." Grandma Em's voice was compassionate.

Realizing she hadn't thought of it that way, Abby looked away. It was certainly the way she was acting.

"Can I ask you something, Abby?" Grandma Em waited until the younger woman's attention was focused on her and then said in a gentle way, "When is a good time for your husband to die? Is it when he's young and the two of you have your whole life ahead of you? How about after you have children and you need him there when they're sick and to help you raise them up God's way? Or maybe it's better after the children are gone and you're ready for some peaceful years spent watching your grandchildren grow with him by your side?"

Grandma Em turned away then and looked at some distant point out the window. "Or did you think the best time was when you were old and you've both lived a full life and your faces are no longer beautiful but seamed with the lines of time? Did you think that was the best time, Abby, when it's been you and him as one for over 45 years?" She turned from her study out the window then and met Abby's eyes straight on. "Believe me, Abby, there is no good time for your mate to die."

Abby sank slowly into a kitchen chair and looked at nothing for a few seconds. "I want to talk with him," she whispered, and Grandma Em knew she wasn't really being addressed. "I want to tell him one more time that I love him. I want him to hold me and tell me all is going to be fine." Tears were brimming in Grandma Em's eyes, but the young widow at the table was dry-eyed.

Grandma Em suspected there was a determination and strength of character that no one would suspect just looking at Abby. In fact, to look at Abby with her mass of dark-red, curly hair and huge, silver-gray eyes, one just wanted to protect her. Her nose was slightly tilted at the end and had just a sprinkling of freckles. All of it effected an aura of innocence.

Her lovely facial features atop a short but quite rounded figure was more than a little eye-catching. But it was obvious the only eyes this young woman wanted to catch were now closed in death. And Grandma Em knew that only Abby's faith in God and time were going to heal that hurt. She said a quick prayer of thanksgiving that Abby knew Jesus Christ, for Grandma Em knew from experience that He would be her everything.

Abby was not sure of anything as the two women continued working on breakfast. Everything inside of her hurt, but she had to go on even with the pain. She had promised. But then, God had promised too.

Abby was reminded of one of God's promises after breakfast when Grandma Em reached for her Bible. "Isaiah 26, verses 3 and 4," she read, "Thou wilt keep him in perfect peace, whose mind is stayed on thee, because he trusteth in thee. Trust ye in the Lord for ever, for in the Lord Jehovah is everlasting strength."

They were words that would help to sustain Abby throughout the day. She realized she had been walking around in a daze since she arrived in Baxter. So when Grandma Em mentioned she was working on a list for downtown, Abby offered to go and then waited patiently for the list. She tried to read the list over to see if she had any questions, but Grandma Em said the beauty of the day was waiting and she should start right out.

Abby couldn't help but agree with Grandma Em about the weather as she headed into downtown Baxter. She found the stores charming and was greeted with smiles everywhere. Abby's last stop, before going over to say hello to Maggie, was the general store.

She methodically went through the list, piling the things on the counter: "black thread, six black buttons, garden gloves, garden trowel, two boxes of matches, crackers, rice, yeast cakes, coffee, pepper, and bright spring fabric for a dress for Abby."

Abby stopped short in the middle of the store as if she had run into a wall. She reread the last item:

> bright spring
> fabric for a
> dress for Abby

The note had a postscript: "And if you don't come home with something, Abby, we'll head right back to town."

Abby couldn't believe she hadn't noticed this, but Grandma Em had written the list with just a few words on each line. At a glance, the last item looked like a continuation of supplies.

Abby looked surreptitiously down at her dress. It wasn't at all becoming. It was an awful shade of brown and made her think of swamp mud. One of the women in the church at Bruce Mines had given it to her, and Abby had altered it herself. She knew the dress had bothered Ian because he didn't have the money to buy her something better, but she had so little to wear that she had been thankful for it even though it was such a ghastly color.

Ian wouldn't have wanted her to mourn him. He would have been thrilled for her to have a new dress. With this thought in mind, she walked over to the fabric counter. Abby stood for a moment looking up at the beautiful colors, when a young girl moved to wait on her. Having an eye for color, the girl reached almost immediately for a soft, light-gray percale. Abby fingered the fabric with something akin to awe.

"I thought it would make a pretty dress, one that would go with your eyes." The girl spoke almost shyly.

"How did you know I wanted dress material?" Abby asked in surprise. She was further bemused when the girl blushed furiously.

"I saw your list when you set it on the counter." The girl didn't raise her eyes until she heard a soft laugh. Abby then noticed a woman whose resemblance marked her as the girl's mother moving toward them.

She spoke good-naturedly. "I promise you Tina wasn't being nosey. It's a little trick I taught her to help customers. If we know what people want, we can serve them better."

"Grandma Em's like that," the girl spoke now, referring back to the list. "If she's decided you're to have a new dress, then you'll have a new dress."

Abby smiled at her confidence, and the girl moved for the box of patterns.

Leaving the store some 20 minutes later for Dr. Cameron's house, Abby felt like she had been run over by a train. A new dress—it had been a long time. If only Ian could see it.

9

Walking back to Grandma Em's, Abby tried to repeat the verses she had heard that morning and prayed for strength. She had not meant to stay long visiting her aunt but had ended up having lunch with Maggie and the Camerons.

Seeing Mark and Susanne Cameron, obviously very happy and in love with each other and their children, sent an ache through her that would just not go away.

The Cameron children were darling, and Abby had fallen quickly under the spell of four-month-old Ellen. Abby would have taken her in a minute.

The slightest look of uncertainty flickered across Grandma Em's eyes when Abby arrived, causing Abby to remember the dress material. Abby instantly opened the parcel.

"The young girl at the store helped me choose. Do you think it will be okay?"

Grandma Em smoothed the fabric and then held it beneath Abby's chin. The effect was stunning. "It will be lovely on you," she stated simply. To have expressed how truly gorgeous the dress would look would have been lost right now on this young widow.

"Thank you for the dress. I'll admit to you, I haven't had a new one in a long time, and I really appreciate your thoughtfulness."

"You are more than welcome, Abby. I assure you it was my pleasure. You had enough money?"

"Good" was all she said at Abby's nod. "Did you have lunch? I assume you ate with Maggie and the family."

"Yes, I hope I didn't hold you up."

"Not in the least. Now I'm in the mood to sew! If you're up to it, I think we should make that dress."

Abby stared at her in surprise, but Grandma Em was carrying things into the kitchen. Knowing herself to be only a fair seamstress, Abby was glad to have the help. What Abby didn't know was that Grandma Em had a funny feeling that Abby was not going to be in Baxter very long and wanted the dress done before God moved this young woman out of her care.

The two women worked well through the afternoon, and the dress was shaping up nicely by supper. Maggie had planned to join them, but when she was over half an hour late, they ate without her.

"She and Mark must be busy today," Grandma Em commented.

"I think you're right. They were involved with a patient when I got there today, and Dr. Cameron didn't linger over lunch."

"It seems like every woman in town is expecting."

"Your family certainly doesn't lack for little ones."

"You're right about that. Having them all pregnant and then deliver within three months was almost more than some of us could take—and all girls to boot. The last year has been anything but boring."

"I can't remember the other babies' names," Abby said a bit apologetically.

"Well, it isn't any wonder. You met everyone who's home on the same day. Luke is oldest and married to Christine. They have Josh and now baby Kathrine. They named her after Luke's mother.

"Mark is a few minutes younger than Luke, and you know all of them." Abby answered in the affirmative, and Grandma Em went on.

"Silas is after the twins, and his wife is Amy. They've been married less than a year and right now are over visiting Amy's father in Neillsville.

"Next is Julia and her husband, Mac. They have Calvin and Charlie, and their new little one is Robyn. The youngest in the family is Paul."

Abby, usually so sensitive to expressions and moods, missed the quietness in Grandma Em's voice as she finished with Paul's name.

"Paul's not married?"

"He's a widower."

There was no missing the grief this time, and Abby was sorry she had asked.

They washed up the dishes and were moving into the living room when Maggie arrived. She and the doctor had in fact been delivering a baby, and she said she was too tired to be hungry.

The evening was not a long one. Soon after Maggie left, Abby made her way to her room. As always, she lay thinking of Ian, missing him and hoping tomorrow would bring some relief.

10

Standing in front of the full-length mirror in Grandma Em's bedroom, Abby stared at her reflection. The dress was finished and fit Abby to perfection. Stylish yet simple, the day dress was very flattering. The bodice had side pleats and a row of white buttons down the middle. Grandma Em had produced a beautiful hand-laced collar from a chest in her room, and Abby's hand went up to finger the delicate lace at the high neck. The sleeves were three-quarter length and puffed at the shoulder. The gray fabric with the white touches on the neck and bodice was gorgeous. Grandma Em watched Abby's face and could see she was both pleased and chagrined.

"It is really lovely. I just somehow hoped I would look thinner."

It suddenly all became very clear to Grandma Em—Abby's always refusing dessert and rarely taking second helpings. She was not fat, but then neither was she a broom handle. Her waist was small, but her hips and bust were quite full. Grandma Em was sure that her roundness, along with her marked lack of height, had probably been a trial to her most of her life.

"I agree with you. It is lovely, and your figure is just fine."

Abby was not going to argue with this woman who had probably never had an ounce of spare flesh in her life. The dress was pretty, and most of the time Abby accepted the way she was shaped. Ian had thought her beautiful. "Don't think of it, Abby," she told herself as she turned away to thank Grandma Em.

"I can see you don't believe me," Grandma Em spoke before she could. "But you really do look wonderful—face, figure, and all."

Abby couldn't help but smile. "You don't miss anything, do you?"

Grandma Em laughed at this, and then both women heard the front door open. "Gram?"

Grandma Em turned and hurried down the stairs with Abby on her heels. She was sure that was Silas' voice, but she didn't think he and Amy were due back yet.

Silas was indeed at the bottom of the stairs and gave her a long hug once she reached him. Without speaking, Silas broke the hug and led his grandmother to the sofa. Amy was sitting in the chair, and the serious look on her face gave Grandma Em the first signal of alarm.

"Silas, what's happened?"

"It's Paul," he told her directly. "We think he's been in an accident. Both legs broken and possibly his arm."

Silas felt her hand tremble in his, but her voice was strong. "Tell me everything. And Abby," she spoke to the young woman lingering uncertainly on the stairs, "come in and sit down. This is Abby, Maggie's niece."

Normally Abby would have balked at intruding on such a personal matter, but she felt no rejection from Silas or Amy, only concern for Paul.

"While we were at the farm, Amy's dad received a letter. It was from a man he worked with years ago, before he bought the farm."

Grandma Em watched as Silas pulled a folded letter from his pocket. "He said we could bring it with us. The man is one of the mill owners in Hayward. Near the end of the letter he says, 'I'd heard your daughter married a Cameron. We have a Cameron laid up here—both legs broke, possibly his arm or wrist. There is no one here to care for him, and he's in a bad way. There have been so many of these boys over the years, I'm not sure why I even mentioned it. It's just that I was at the camp, and he was in the bunkhouse alone and in a lot of pain. On the chance he's one of yours, I was sure you'd want to know.'"

Silas was sick at having to tell his grandmother in this way. He glanced at his wife and could see she knew what he was feeling.

"The letter you received—he said he was in Hayward?"

"Yes."

Grandma Em looked grief-stricken, and across the room Abby felt helpless.

"I could leave in the morning," Silas said. "I'll go and see if it's him and bring him home."

"Does the letter say anything about how long he's been hurt?" The enormity of what had happened to her grandson was quickly closing in on her, and Grandma Em could barely speak. She was beginning to feel ill as she pictured Paul hurt, helpless, and alone.

Instantly Abby was at her side easing her back on the sofa and placing a small pillow beneath her head. Grandma Em felt her legs being lifted.

"I need a glass of water and a blanket, please."

Grandma Em looked up to see that it was Abby speaking, but she had never heard that tone of voice from her before. A strong arm supported her. "It's just water. Sip it. That's good. Now close your eyes. Try to take slow, even breaths."

"I can't stand it, knowing he's hurt. . . ."

"I know," Abby's voice was soothing. "It's worse when he's so far away and you can't take care of him."

"Abby," Grandma Em grasped the younger woman's hand as she made a snap decision, her voice stronger now, her eyes pleading with Abby's. "Abby, will you go? Will you go up and take care of Paul? I know he won't welcome the family; he left here so bitter. I can't stand knowing he's up there by himself."

Abby was stunned. Did this woman know what she was asking? There was no telling how Paul was doing now or if it really was Paul. The nurse in her thought of all the possibilities—the infections, gangrene, pneumonia. The list was a long one. He could be dead before she arrived—or even now.

She knew she had to be honest. "Mrs. Cameron, I don't think you realize the seriousness of this."

"I know what you're going to say, and you're wrong. I do realize the seriousness. I was married to a doctor for over 45 years." Abby stared at Grandma Em, seeing how little she knew about her. "The man in the letter is Paul and he's not dead." Her voice was growing stronger. She wanted to sit up, and Abby helped her.

"I'm certain that he's not dead, Abby. Yesterday when you were in town, I prayed and prayed that you would bring that dress material. I felt God was telling me you would not be here for very long, and I wanted you to have the dress before you left. I'll admit I didn't think it would be this soon, but I've prayed for Paul every day of his life, and right now he has emotional hurts—deep emotional hurts. Those he'll have to deal with on his own, but you're qualified to take care of him physically. I think you're an answer to prayer for Paul's needs, and I'm asking you to go."

Abby would have loved to walk out of the living room and pretend she hadn't heard any of this. "Will you give me some time to pray?" Abby asked, trying to right a world that suddenly felt like it was spinning.

Her eyes tearing, Grandma Em reached for and hugged Abby. The young widow returned the hug and then made her way upstairs, knowing as she did she would soon be leaving for Hayward.

11

By supper time of the same day, the entire family had been informed of the situation. Each person made their way to Abigail at one time or another and thanked her—Luke and Julia with tears in their eyes.

The women convened the following morning and two more dresses, undergarments, and a nightgown were quickly sewn for Abby. Christine brought a few articles of clothing Paul had left at the house. Fabric and patterns were added so Abby could sew for Paul if necessary. Mark tried to guess what medical things Abby would need, and they were added to the pile of things to go in the trunk that would accompany Abby to the north woods.

"You're sure about this, Abby?" her aunt asked her when they had a private moment together.

"I won't tell you I'm not scared, but I'm sure God wants me to go. I had hoped to find work and stay close to you for a while."

"I would have loved it, but like you said, God is sending you, so I'm sure He'll give us time together at a later date. Paul's a good man, but as broken as his body must be, his heart is hurting far more. You go and see to his needs, and we'll write like we always have. You know I'll be praying."

The entire family pitched in and tried to second-guess any surprises for Abby. Less than 48 hours after Silas and Amy brought the letter from Neillsville, Abby was at the train station.

Mac was busy with his fields, but he felt very strongly about taking Abby to the train station and insisted on being the one to pick her and Grandma Em up and see them there.

The three sat at the station with Abby's trunk nearby and Mac began to question her as a father would upon sending his daughter away.

"You have plenty of money?"

"I'm sure I do," she answered, thinking of the money Luke had given her. She had never had so much in her life.

"Is there anything else you can think of?"

"No, everyone has given more than enough."

"I want to tell you something, Abby. The last time I saw Paul, he was so angry and bitter I hardly recognized him, but that's not the Paul I've always known. It was Paul, when he was just a boy, who led me to my understanding of Jesus Christ and all He did for me.

"So you see, he holds a special place in my heart. We'll be praying you find a place to live and that you have enough money. I feel sure that God will put Paul back on his feet. When he does, will you please encourage him to come home, even for just a visit? We so want to see Paul, and if you can get him on his feet and send him or bring him this way, well, I can't begin to tell you what it would mean."

Mac looked at the small woman on the bench beside him. Her strength and determination reminded him of his Julia. She was the type of girl he hoped his boys would grow up and marry. He had to say one more thing. "In the excitement over Paul, you may be thinking we've forgotten you. We haven't." Abby could see Grandma Em's head moving in agreement as she listened to Mac.

"We all know how fresh your hurt is. You can go, knowing that back in Baxter, the MacDonalds and the Camerons are praying for you every day."

They sat the rest of the wait in silence. Soon the ground was rumbling with the movement of the incoming train.

Memories of arriving less than a month ago assailed Abby, and she laughed a little. Both Mac and Grandma Em stared at her. She knew she had to explain.

"When you came toward me the day I first arrived, I was terrified of you."

"I know," Mac said with a grin.

Abby smiled back. "I thought you must eat small red-heads for breakfast."

"No, only at afternoon tea."

The light banter helped ease the minds of Grandma Em and Abby. All of Grandma Em's grandchildren had come to her and offered to go to Paul, either with Abby or alone. But in talking together, they agreed that a nonmember of the family would be better at this time.

Abby was not a woman easily intimidated, so going alone did not frighten her. Her greatest worry was having to come back and tell this special family that their loved one was dead. The smell of death was too fresh in her nostrils, and she wasn't sure if she was more afraid for the family or for herself.

12

The days of trusting God were over. Paul Cameron believed he would plot his own course now, because he could certainly do a better job than God had done recently. Paul knew the thought to be irreverent, blasphemous even, but the anger and bitterness that grew with every mile he moved away from Baxter overrode him. He gave into that sin of angry bitterness without a fight—not even a whimper.

Now, weeks after leaving his grandmother's home, Paul walked alone into the woods at the start of a new day. It didn't matter that the sun was breaking clear and bright over the land; miles and miles of gigantic pine trees cast darkness over everything.

As Paul walked, he noted absently his arms and legs no longer screamed in agony from a day of cutting logs. Not that he minded the pain in his body—it helped dull the pain in his heart.

The other ninety-odd men heading into the "pineries," a nickname for the massive stretches of pine trees in the Wisconsin north woods, steered clear of Paul. He had worn an expression in the cook tent at breakfast that told them he was not in a mood for jokes.

From the first moment he arrived in camp, Paul's height had made him stand out. With the help of the logging trade, the breadth of his chest, along with the way the muscles bulged in his arms made him a man only the foolish would challenge or even speak to if Paul's mood was wrong.

Generally he was well-liked in camp. He could drink with the best of them, and he never cheated at cards—parting with his hard-earned money better than most. His living habits were clean, and he always pulled more than his weight on any job.

Paul was careful in not getting too close to anyone. The men he worked with knew nothing about him, so they had no way of knowing that this morning's mood stemmed from a dream about Corrine—not the smiling, beautiful Corrine of the first few days of courtship, but the Corrine of the last days, pale as the sheets she lay on, so still and near death. . . . Paul shoved the thoughts aside and continued on into the trees.

Paul's family would have been hard put to recognize the man he had become. His hair was long, obviously having not seen a barber since he'd left Baxter, and a full, dark beard covered his face. But the biggest change was in Paul's personality. Gone was the carefree youth with the sparkling blue eyes with whom they had grown up. Gone was the dedicated man of God they had watched him become. In his place was an angry, bitter man who believed his life was over because he felt dead inside.

There wasn't a day that passed when Paul did not hear the voice of God beckoning to him. Paul was fast becoming proficient at pushing such thoughts aside and going about as he pleased. However, he had promised his grandmother he would stay in touch. So upon arriving and getting work in the logging camp, he had written her a brief note.

"Gram," it stated simply, "I'm on a logging crew in Hayward. Please do not watch for me. It's going to be a long time, if ever, before my road leads home again. Paul."

Paul had no way of knowing that his grandmother held that letter in her hand every day and prayed for him, and that many nights as the moon flooded through the window in her bedroom, she would fall asleep looking at it on her bedside table.

In the back of Paul's mind he was quite sure God would grow weary of his willful behavior. When this happened, he assumed God would end his life upon the earth. As hard as his heart was, the thought was a sobering one. But Paul, in his own strength, could not bring himself to deal with the seriousness of his sin, and he refused to call on God for help.

Paul, in his sureness of how God would deal with him, was totally unprepared for the severe blow about to be dealt him that very day.

Sweat ran freely from every pore of Paul's body several hours later as he and his partner worked in perfect rhythm on either end of a crosscut saw.

Paul's partner slowed near the end of the cut and, as the men moved away from the falling tree, Paul rounded on him in a burst of angry impatience.

"Were you taking a nap over there? I'm sick of doing all the work. If you're going to cut logs with me, then you . . ."

One instant Paul was shouting and the next he was being pitched through the air as the top of the tree they just felled lashed back and caught him below the knees.

He awoke not many minutes later to shouts and agony. Both legs were broken and his arm was twisted beneath him at an odd angle. He was lying facedown a good ten feet from where he had been standing. Even through the pain, he knew he wasn't going to die.

It wasn't supposed to be like this. He was supposed to die—not get hurt and crippled. God's plans had been different than his own. Paul told himself he had been betrayed again.

"Nooooo." Paul's scream of agony was directed at God.

Getting ready to lift him onto a horse for the ride back to camp, the men ignored him. When a man was busted up, the pain could make him crazy. They all breathed a sigh of relief when five men dropped him facedown over the horse's back and he passed out.

13

Abigail stood on the train station platform and surveyed what she could see of Hayward. It looked to be a small but busy town. The dirt streets were alive with activity, and Abby was a bit disheartened to see so many men. She had half expected as much when she found out she was headed into the heart of logging country. Well, she told herself, she had a job to do and God was with her. Nothing was going to keep her from her task.

Abby held her small bag a little closer as she thought of the letters within. There were two of them. One *to* a Mr. Sam Beckett and the other *from* Mr. Sam Beckett. He was the man who had written to Amy's father. Amy had written on behalf of her father in case Abby arrived before his letter did. Silas had suggested she bring the original letter as a way of introducing herself to Mr. Beckett.

It was at that moment that Abby was distracted from her reflections to realize she was attracting attention. Disheveled and dusty as she was, she was still drawing quite a few looks—or rather, her hair was. Too late she realized her bonnet was hanging down her back.

Once the strings were tied and everything back in place, Abby felt safe. But one bold young man—Abby guessed him to be about 16 or 17—sauntered over and stopped directly in front of her.

He bent slightly to peek beneath the brim and spoke. "I don't suppose you'd care to take your hat back off, would ya?"

Abby did not even disdain to answer him, but leveled him with a disapproving look. She would have liked to box his ears for accosting a decent woman in broad daylight. But her look did not phase him. He pinned on his most winning smile and spoke again.

"Now ma'am, I can see you're suspicious of my request, but the truth is, your hair is the color of my own sainted mother's back home, and it makes me feel a might comforted just to look at it."

Abby had the urge to laugh outright. He was a charming liar. Abby took a closer look. He was nice-looking and his clothing was well-cut, making her think his family probably had money. The face watching her so intently was smooth and boyish. His hair was a nice sandy brown, and even in his teens he topped Abby by many inches. He probably thought her younger than her 23 years.

"I don't suppose you could help me with my trunk?" Abby said sweetly, trying another tactic.

The boy's smile stretched to his ears. "Oh yes, ma'am, I'd be glad to help."

Abby caught movement beyond the young man and noticed three other boys of approximately the same age watching every move of their exchange. She was sure the one before her had come over on a bet.

"I'm headed to Mr. Sam Beckett's home and I need some help...."

"Sam Beckett?"

Abby smiled to herself. She had hoped Mr. Beckett was a man of at least some importance in this town, and judging from the boy's reaction, her wish had come true. The boy looked almost ill. All smiles were gone, and he was casting apprehensive looks over his shoulder to his comrades.

"Yes," Abby continued, all sweetness and light, "Mr. Sam Beckett. If you could just get my trunk and show me to where he lives, I'd be very grateful."

"Actually, I just remembered I can't. That is, I have something else I need to do." Gone was the lazy drawl he had been addressing her with earlier. Here stood a frustrated and embarrassed young man. Jamming the hat he had been mutilating back on his head, he nearly ran to escape her.

Abby ended up leaving her trunk within the tidy little

station office for safekeeping and, after receiving directions to the Beckett home, started on her way.

Standing on the street outside the Beckett home, Abby thought her heart would hammer through her skin. It was an imposing structure: two stories of fresh paint and gleaming panes of glass. She prayed for strength and wisdom as she approached the door.

Abby had half expected a servant to answer, but somehow she knew immediately that the kind-looking woman before her, in a well-cut dress and lovely hairstyle, was Mrs. Beckett.

"I'm looking for Mr. Sam Beckett. Would he be at home?"

"Are you looking for work?" the woman asked.

"No, I'm here on a personal matter."

The woman looked at her strangely, and Abby didn't blame her. How would she have felt if some woman had come looking for Ian on a "personal matter"?

Nevertheless, she was allowed to enter and asked to wait in the foyer. Abby's eyes skipped quickly over the large entryway. The walls and woodwork were painted white, and the rug, in golds and browns, looked imported. It wasn't long before she heard heavy footsteps approaching.

"Mr. Beckett," Abby spoke as he approached and at the same time dug in her bag for the letters, "my name is Abigail Finlayson, and I'm here about a letter you wrote to Grant Nolan."

Abby gave him a moment to recognize the letter, and then handed him the one addressed to him from Amy. She studied him silently as he read. He was of medium height with a robust frame. She figured he was in his mid to late 40's. He looked very much like the serious businessman he must have been to be a mill owner—and a successful one at that—if his home was any indication.

"Please, Mrs. Finlayson, come in and meet my wife." He broke suddenly into Abby's study of him and led her into a lovely parlor where she was introduced briefly to the woman who had opened the front door: Lenore Beckett.

"Will you excuse us for a moment, Mrs. Finlayson?"

Abby was not given time to answer before both husband and wife left and took the two letters with them.

As in the foyer, the walls of the parlor were painted white, making everything look immaculate and elegant. Abby's chair was near the fireplace where above the mantle was a portrait of a stern-looking woman.

Two doors led off the room and, knowing one led back to the foyer, Abby couldn't help but wonder where the other one led. As always, in the back of Abby's mind was the wish that Ian could be here sharing in all of this. But then, she reminded herself, she probably would not be here if Ian were still alive.

Abby felt suddenly tired of being alone. To think he had only been gone a few short weeks, and she had the rest of her life to think about and picture him at her side. She may have talked herself into a good cry, one she had not yet indulged in, but the lady of the house entered the room from the mystery door and Mr. Beckett was with her.

After they were seated, Mr. Beckett spoke. "We're very glad you came to us, Mrs. Finlayson. The truth is, my wife knew nothing of the young man I saw out at the camp until I just now told her. She is very softhearted, and we would have a constant stream of injured men here if she knew of all the incidents.

"We'd like to help you in any way we can. It's true that Grant and I go back a long way and, according to Amy's letter, you're just about family. Can you tell us what you had in mind?"

Abby wanted to sing, her heart was so full of thanksgiving to God and the way He was taking care of her. He was providing friendship and support in these people when she felt so alone. Surely they would help her find a place to stay and men to help her move Paul. She carefully mapped out her plan to the Becketts.

"I have my doubts that Mr. Cameron is going to want to come with me, so I plan to hire men to take him from the bunkhouse. He is still there?" Abby asked, afraid of the answer.

"Yes, he is. I couldn't get him off my mind, and I was over to check on him just this week." Mr. Beckett ignored the look his wife sent him that said she felt he was as soft as she.

"Good. I plan to find places for us to stay this afternoon. I can get myself settled in and have him moved to his place tomorrow."

"We want you both to stay with us," Mrs. Beckett interrupted in a rush. "The letter said you are a nurse and that you're here to take care of Paul Cameron and get him back on his feet. Well, I think you can do that right here. There is an empty bedroom right here on the first floor off the kitchen where Mr. Cameron can stay. Our daughter is grown and moved out, and you can have her room upstairs."

Abby could only stare at the woman. She couldn't believe what she was hearing, but she knew she had to be honest with these people. "Your offer is more than I could have hoped for, but I think you need to know about Mr. Cameron. His family was afraid to come up because the last they saw of him he was very angry and bitter.

"I don't think he's going to react appreciatively in his helpless state to my coming in and moving him, probably causing him a lot of pain, to someplace I can take care of him when he hasn't even asked for my help.

"I'm not afraid of the task, but I want you to be aware of the possible interruption to your home."

To Abby's surprise, they were both smiling at her. Mr. Beckett's voice was cheerful as he spoke. "I'm not surprised to find you're not afraid of the job ahead of you. My guess is you're not afraid of anything," he said with approval.

"We're not worried about any disruption in our home. You're welcome to stay as long as you need." Mr. Beckett was tempted to ask her what her husband thought of all this, but kept the question to himself.

They continued to talk for a time and make plans. Abby and Mrs. Beckett were on a first-name basis within minutes. Lenore assured her she would have their son, Ross, pick up the trunk from the station.

Abby discussed with Mr. Beckett the best way to move Paul. Before she had time to think, they were headed out to the camp with four extra men to bring Paul Cameron into town, with or without his approval.

14

"Maybe you shouldn't come with us, Mrs. Finlayson. It's not very clean."

"Thank you, Mr. Beckett, but I'll be fine." Abby nearly regretted her words a few minutes later.

Bunk beds lined the walls of the empty building. It was obvious the men had been gone for a good while, but the stale smell of smoke and unwashed bodies lingered.

The six people skirted the stove in the middle of the room and moved toward the rear. Paul Cameron was on a lower bunk at the back, and Abby was horrified at his condition of neglect. His beard and hair were matted with food, and his body and union suit reeked of sweat and human waste. Abby was sure the blankets he lay on had not been cleaned or aired since he had been placed upon them. A hand to Paul's bearded cheek told Abby there was no fever. He didn't stir when she touched him.

Directing the men to take the four corners of the blanket, Abby had them lift him carefully from the bunk. It was enough to bring Paul around, and the first person he spotted was Abby.

"What are you doing? Put me down!" His voice was a bit rusty from lack of use, but he spoke with force.

Abby had decided long ago she was not going to have an argument with this man, and an explanation now would surely cause one. She ignored the question.

The men began to walk now, and Paul realized he was being moved from the building. "What are you doing? Put me down!" Paul spoke with enough command to check the men in their stride.

"Put him in the wagon." Abby spoke in a no-nonsense voice that propelled the men forward without question.

Paul opened his mouth to tell this woman what he thought of her high-handedness, but the men at the foot of the blanket moved wrong and Paul felt nauseous from the pain.

Gritting his teeth to keep from screaming when they put him in the wagon, Paul didn't recognize any of his bearers and never caught sight of Mr. Beckett, who was driving the wagon.

Paul's entire body convulsed in agony as the wagon dropped into the ruts in the road. As spots danced before his eyes, he knew he couldn't take much more. His last thought before darkness invaded was that he wanted to murder the redhead bending over him.

Paul's bedroom had obviously been a servant's quarters, so furnishings were simple. The bed was large and sat in the middle of one wall. There were two windows, and Abby could see the shadows lengthening with the setting of the sun.

A washstand stood in one corner along with a small wardrobe. Wooden pegs on the wall held Paul's few things which Mr. Beckett had carried from the bunkhouse. On the far side of the bed was a small table with a lantern and on the other side was a rocking chair in which Abby sat, watching her sleeping patient.

Washed now and with fresh splints, Paul lay in a clean bed. Abby couldn't remember ever feeling so tired, but the sense of accomplishment more than made up for it.

Even though the temptation was overwhelming, she had not cut his hair for fear of igniting his fury. He had been angry enough as it was. Coming to from time to time, Paul ordered her hands off him or swore at her. Abby had ignored it all and scrubbed him from head to foot.

Movement beyond the door reminded Abby that the Becketts had a cook who lived in town and came each day to the house. She knew it was getting close to supper. Abby only hoped she would be able to stay awake.

"I can't think what has become of Ross. He dropped your trunk off and I haven't seen him since." Lenore was more than a little upset with her son at the supper table later. "I wish you would speak to him, Sam. He knows when we eat supper."

"I'll talk to him, dear."

"Abby, did you get a chance to settle into your room?"

"No, I didn't get more than a quick peek. It is really lovely, though."

"If there is anything you need, just ask."

Abby smiled and thought that the only thing she needed was sleep.

The dishes were being cleared when the front door opened. The dining room door that led to the parlor was open, as was the door leading out into the foyer. The absentee son didn't stand a chance of entering unheard.

"Ross, come into the dining room, please." Sam Beckett's voice carried easily to the entryway.

Abby's mouth nearly dropped open and some of her exhaustion disappeared when the young man from the train depot walked through the door.

Abby listened with only half an ear to the exchange between father and son as she recalled how upset he had been at the mention of the Beckett name. Her attention returned at the sound of her name.

"Abby, this is our son, Ross. Ross, this is Abigail Finlayson. She and a man who is in her care will be staying with us for a while."

Abby took instant pity on the red-faced youth. His eyes didn't plead with her, but Abby was sure he was holding his breath.

"It's a pleasure to meet you, Ross."

His sigh was audible and his smile was back in charming force as he repeated the amenities. Ross was then ordered by his mother into the kitchen for his supper.

Abby made her apologies, checked on Paul, and took herself off to bed. Her last prayerful supplication as she fell into a dreamless sleep was that all her days in Hayward would not be this busy.

15

Abby had checked on Paul twice during the night and found him sleeping. She made sure the bedpan was within reach and, other than those short visits to see to his needs, slept through the night.

Ready to take on anything the next morning, she began her day in the Scriptures. In Luke 11, starting with verse 33, she read, "No man, when he hath lighted a candle, putteth it in a secret place, neither under a bushel, but on a candlestick, that they who come in may see the light."

As soon as Abby read the words, she thought of the promise. With an effort, she didn't cry. It wasn't that she planned to break her word, it was just that she never believed she would be alone to carry it out.

Dear heavenly Father, Ian is with You now, and I know this was Your will. I hurt. I hurt so much. You gave him to me. He was the husband of Your choice, and now You have seen fit to take him home to Yourself. Please hold me close, Lord. Comfort me with Your Word. And please, Lord, help me keep my promise.

Abby washed and dressed and thought about being a light to the Becketts. She prayed again and asked God to give her opportunities to share Him.

Her next thoughts were of Paul. In the confusion of leaving Baxter, she had not slowed anyone down long enough to ask a few questions about Paul. Her aunt must have known something, but when they talked she hadn't elaborated.

He was a widower—she knew that much. And Grandma Em had made it sound like he was angry with the family, or maybe his bitterness was directed at God and that made him angry with everyone.

The subject of Abby's thoughts was just waking up in his downstairs bedroom. As usual, Paul's first thoughts were of Corrine. It was getting harder and harder to picture her laughing or smiling at him with eyes of love. The time he had seen her that way had been so short; their total time together had been all too brief.

He wished he had understood the severity of her illness. It wouldn't have changed his feelings, but the surprise was so hard to take. She shouldn't have died. There was no reason for her to die. God could have healed her so easily; He could have reached down and lengthened her life for many years. After all, their plans to work for Him were so big, so wonderful. Paul let the now-familiar feelings of betrayal wash over him.

Some minutes passed before he allowed himself to come out of his tiny shell of misery. Where in the world was he? Oh yes, he smiled unkindly—the bossy redhead. At the same time that Paul remembered the woman herself, he remembered her bathing him. A fast look under the sheet told him his worst fears had come true. He was wearing only his leg splints and a bandage on his wrist. "Well," he thought uncharitably, "at least I can stand my own stench for the first time in weeks."

The bedroom door opened on his bitter mood, and the present object of his anger walked confidently toward the bed.

"Good morning, Mr. Cameron. Did you sleep well?"

"Where am I?" Paul growled without answering her.

"You're in the home of Mr. Sam Beckett."

It was not the answer Paul had expected, and it gave him pause. Beckett was one of the mill owners and for some reason had come to see him twice in the bunkhouse. Why would he move him here? Surely he had better things to do with his time than take care of one of the many loggers who was injured.

Paul felt no better after having run all this through his mind, and his voice was no less curt on his next question. "Who are you?"

"I'm your nurse, and my name is Mrs. Finlayson." Abby's voice was kind, but she did not offer any more information than necessary.

Now Paul was really confused. Why would Sam Beckett bring him here and hire a nurse to take care of him? He thought of asking the woman by his bed, but she was just hired help and he doubted she would know.

Paul felt at a definite disadvantage next to her. She was calm in answering his questions and she could come and go as she pleased, whereas Paul knew he was nearly help-less and undressed to boot.

"Where are my clothes?"

"The ones with you in the bunkhouse are hanging over on the pegs. The ones you were wearing were not savable."

"What do you mean by 'not savable'?"

"I burned them."

"You what?" he exploded at her. "What gives you the right to . . ."

Paul stopped shouting when he realized she wasn't even listening to him. Abby had walked over to the windows to draw open the curtains and to let in a little air. She took her time and, when everything was straightened to her liking, she went back to stand by the bed.

"Would you like some breakfast?" When Paul only stared at her in open hostility, she continued. "I'll go now and fix your breakfast. I won't be long."

Abby reached without embarrassment and touched the bedpan. She waited until his eyes followed her hand before exiting without another word.

Paul had never known such humiliation and anger. He pic-tured himself throwing the bedpan at her retreating back, but didn't follow through with the violent thought. With eyes focused bleakly on the ceiling above, he knew without a doubt he was living in a nightmare of his own making.

16

Abby closed the bedroom door and leaned against it. He was not happy and she suspected he was feeling violent, but he hadn't thrown anything at her. It wouldn't have been the first time. Abby thought wryly of her days in the hospital with some of the most unpredictable patients a nurse could *never* hope to meet.

Before she had gone into the bedroom, she had stoked the fire and put on some coffee. With a little searching she had all she needed and was well on her way. Abby was just finishing with the tray when in walked the cook. In her middle years, she was short and stocky with blonde hair and blue eyes set in pale features.

"Hello! I stoked the fire and started the coffee. I have to deliver this tray and then I'll be back."

The woman smiled broadly at her, bobbing her head but not saying a word. Feeling a bit bemused, Abby picked up the tray and moved to the bedroom.

"Well now, that didn't take too long, but you must be hungry." Abby shifted the table a little nearer to the bed and set the tray down. She felt Paul's eyes on her as she moved to the wardrobe and removed two pillows she had spotted there yesterday.

"Now if you'll let me, I'll prop these behind you so you can reach the tray."

"I can move myself" was the snarled reply Abby received as she moved to help him.

The nurse watched quietly as her patient placed his palms flat on the bed and attempted to move himself up against the headboard. His bandaged wrist gave out immediately under the pressure, and he glared at Abby as though it were her fault.

"Maybe you'd rather I spoon-fed you," Abby stated in all seriousness. The comment deepened his scowl, but he made no further remarks as she helped him back up against the pillows.

Abby placed the tray across his lap and watched again as he fell on the food as though he were starving. Abby could see why his beard had been matted with food—he ate like a wolf!

"I'll be right out the door here, in the kitchen. Call if you need anything." A grunt was the only indication he had heard her and Abby exited, thinking she had her work cut out for her.

A little disappointed to see that the cook was gone, Abby poured herself a cup of coffee and sat at the table. Lost in thought over the hostile Mr. Cameron and over possibly getting a letter off to Baxter, Abby soon heard a noise. Turning expectantly and thinking to see the cook approaching, Abby was surprised to see Ross.

"Hello," he greeted her cheerfully as he plopped down in a chair across the table from her. "Boy, was I surprised to come by your room and find the door open and you already up."

"I have a patient to take care of," she told him not unkindly.

"Oh yeah. Who is that guy anyway?"

"His name is Mr. Paul Cameron."

"He's not your husband or anything is he?"

"No," Abby assured him.

"Good."

Abby wondered for a few moments why Ross found this information *good*, but she was too preoccupied to spend much time musing on it.

When she glanced up a few minutes later, it was to find Ross staring intently at her. Warning bells went off in her head and, hoping to remind him he was staring quite rudely, she raised her brows questioningly.

He didn't drop his eyes from hers, but spoke softly. "Why didn't you tell my parents we had talked at the train station?"

Abby shrugged, somewhat relieved that she had misread the look. "I didn't agree with your actions at the train station, but I felt there was no real harm done."

Ross' smile was triumphant. He knew he had been right. She was as attracted to him as he was to her.

Abby frowned at that smile and spoke sternly. "I don't intend to tell your parents of our conversation, Ross, but if I had my way I would have boxed your ears for such behavior."

Ross' triumphant mood evaporated. Why, she was speaking to him as though he were a child! Abby saw the look and interpreted it correctly.

"Ross," her voice was gentle now, "how old are you?"

"I'll be 18 in July." His chest swelled out as he answered.

"You're a man now, Ross, and it was foolish of you to let your friends goad you into that stunt yesterday. I was not amused, and you're old enough to know better."

It was all said so gently, Abby's eyes so filled with kindness, that Ross couldn't find it in himself to be angry. He smiled at her and Abby smiled back, mostly in relief. They had come to an understanding. Had Abby not felt so distracted, she would have noticed Ross' smile was a good deal more personal than her own.

17

"Hey, Red!" The shout came from the bedroom and resounded loudly in the still kitchen.

Abigail's head snapped up and her gray eyes narrowed. Ross' immediate reaction was to laugh, but the fire he saw flashing in Abby's eyes was enough to stifle that sound.

"Excuse me, Ross."

Abby rose stiffly and walked toward the door. Ross watched as she entered the room and shut the door. A huge smile spread across his young face. What a woman!

The door closed, Abby stood just inside and waited for Paul to notice her. It didn't take long.

"Oh, there you are! I'm done with the tray, Red; you can take it away." Abby watched as he lay back against the pillows and closed his eyes with a contented sigh.

Abby held her place, her fury just under the surface. When Paul realized she had not come for the tray, he cocked open one eye and peered at her. "I'm done."

"My name is Mrs. Finlayson."

Paul's head came off the pillow with both eyes open and stared at her. "You sure came fast enough."

"I came in to set you straight about my name. I do not answer to Red." The last word was nearly spit out between clenched teeth.

"Whatever." He didn't seem to notice her anger. "I'm done eating."

Her anger was so great that Abby had to control herself to keep from ripping the pillows out from behind his head. She didn't think she had ever been treated so rudely. Up until now she had taken for granted the respect her profession had afforded.

As Abby worked, she began to look logically at the situation, cooling her anger swiftly as she righted the bed and room. Paul Cameron was a man with a deep hurt. Abby felt for him and whatever that hurt might be, but she could not condone the way he was handling it. Everyone had private pain to live with; she ought to know. But lashing out at God and the world in general was not the answer.

Having taken a few seconds to think this through while she settled Paul back in the bed, Abby could once again address him civilly.

"Mr. Cameron, I'd like to check your wrist." She reached for his arm, but he pulled away.

"It's fine."

"I'd like to see for myself," she countered patiently. And thus the argument went on, Abby calmly holding her ground by the side of the bed and Paul heatedly telling her to get out.

With a movement born of pure frustration, Paul finally thrust his wrist toward her and waited with ill-concealed impatience for her to finish.

Even in his anger he was surprised by her gentleness and watched closely as she unwrapped the wrist and probed the bones carefully with her small hand. Paul felt no pain until she turned his hand a few degrees. He stiffened a moment until he realized she knew of his pain and had immediately stopped.

"Did the doctor tell you it was broken?"

"He never looked at it, and I wasn't awake to tell him it hurt." This explained the strange wrapping of part of an old shirt on the wrist the day before.

"Well, I'm sure it's no more than a bad sprain," she spoke as she expertly rewrapped the wrist. Abby gave Paul no time for objections a moment later when she lifted the covers at the foot of the bed to check his legs.

Her movements were deft and professional, and Paul appreciated her not just throwing the covers off the way the doctor had done to cut off the legs of his union suit. Paul had not been sure what the doctor was going to do but he'd had to wait to find out. As soon as the doctor had touched Paul's legs, he in agony had passed out.

"How bad is the pain?" Abby's quiet voice cut through his thoughts.

"They throb all the time."

"One more than the other?"

"The right more."

Abby paused in her movements and noticed for the first time he was speaking to her in a normal voice and how beautiful that voice was. She also thought him not bad-looking when he wasn't scowling.

When the covers were back in place, Abby spoke. "The breaks are not severe, but the fact that it's both legs will keep you in this bed for a spell. Is there anything you would like? Some books or writing material?"

Paul didn't want her kindness. He resented even needing her help. He answered from behind the wall he had built up around his heart.

"No." His voice was curt. "And don't start nagging on me."

Stung by his words, Abby exited the room with quiet dignity.

18

Abby walked with a weary chuckle to her bedroom. She had gone back into the kitchen, determined to put the hurtful things Paul had said behind her, and had found the Becketts' cook. Abby had jabbered on for who knows how many minutes to her, asking what the wonderful smells were that floated from the stove, praising her neatness, and really attempting to make a friend.

Abby didn't have the slightest inkling as to why the woman had done no more than smile and nod until Lenore had come into the room.

"Abby," she had said kindly, "Anna doesn't speak a word of English."

The whole thing had struck Ross as hilarious as he had followed his mother into the room, and his laughter had almost started Abby's.

Well, she thought, as she entered her bedroom, at least she knew the woman's name and could think of her as more than "the cook." Abby had eaten breakfast and then checked on Paul and found him asleep. As she entered her room, she thought how it was rather nice to have just one patient to care for, finally giving her some free time with which to settle in. And what a beautiful room it was to settle into.

Morning sunlight filtered through two huge windows, and a double bed of a rich red mahogany wood with a full canopy sat against the opposite wall. The rugs, curtains, and bed hangings were all in shades of pink, lavender, and blue. There was a small writing desk and a built-in closet.

Abby attacked her trunk with a vengeance. She filled dresser drawers and hung clothes. The entire room had her things placed about it before she was finished. The last items she put out were a beautiful brush, comb, and mirror set that Ian had given her for her birthday. They had not been able to afford it, and Abby had looked at him with concern until he said he hadn't stolen them and that was all she needed to know.

Abby sank down onto the edge of the bed and pulled the pins from her hair. With her brush she took long, slow strokes, almost wishing the tears would come and hoping they could possibly wash away some of the pain that threatened to choke her.

How long she sat, brushing and softly singing some of the hymns Ian loved she did not know, when there came a knock on the door.

"Who is it?"

"Ross," came the answer from without. Abby, thinking she must be needed, hurried to the door with brush in hand.

"Abby, I was wondering," Ross' voice trailed off slowly as he stood regarding the woman before him. If he had any doubts before, they were gone; he was sure he was in love.

"Ross!" Abby spoke sharply a second time before he dragged his eyes from her unbound hair and only then to stare speechlessly into her eyes.

Abby spun away from the door and grabbed her pins. Within seconds the gorgeous mass of red hair was pinned neatly into place. Abby then returned to the young man still gawking at her from the doorway.

"Ross," Abby's patience had run out, "*what* did you need?"

He recovered quickly and said, "Since you just got here, I thought you might like to take a walk and see some of Hayward."

It was said so sincerely, without the least trace of Ross' usual cockiness, Abby couldn't help but be touched.

"Ross," Abby came into the hallway and shut her door as she answered, "I really appreciate your offer, but I need to stay here in case Mr. Cameron needs anything."

If Abby had expected him to pout over her answer, she was to be disappointed. Ross looked down on her with an expression tender beyond his years and smiled.

"Some other time—okay?"

Abby nodded and watched as he moved down the hall. With her fingers pressing against her temples, her heart felt near the bursting point. His tender look had so reminded her of Ian that she had almost changed her mind about going with him.

"Oh, Lord," Abby prayed, "what am I to do without him?"

19

The days went by and developed into something of a routine. Paul was civil at times, impossible at others. The doctor came over once and told Paul he was progressing well. The man had much praise for Abby and her care of Paul. Paul listened to it all with a bored expression on his face.

Abby worried some about Paul's assumption that Mr. Beckett had been instrumental in bringing him here and hiring Abby. A comment from Paul one day told Abby this was what he thought and she, rather cowardly, had not corrected him.

Abby was not to know the day of reckoning was upon her. Sitting in the kitchen after lunch with a cup of coffee, Abby waited for the barber to emerge from Paul's room. He had quite suddenly asked her if she could get someone to cut his hair.

Abby had been very pleased by the request, not because she cared how he looked, but because of the nice way he had asked her. She felt he was feeling a bit better each day, and his mood improved in kind.

However the surprises were not over that day when Abby paid the barber and saw him on his way. She nearly questioned the price, but figured he must charge more for coming out of his shop. She kept silent, and her curiosity about the cost was answered a few minutes later when she walked into Paul's room.

Paul lay still on the bed, his eyes closed as though the effort of sitting still for the barber had exhausted him. Abby stood by the bed and stared. Not only had the barber cut his hair, but every whisker of Paul's beard was gone. With a start, Abby realized how good-looking he was. Suddenly the picture of the grandchildren and great-grandchildren in Grandma Em's parlor popped into her mind. He had been very handsome in that picture, but his long hair, beard, and the bitter scowl he was always wearing had marred the man Abby met in person.

Here now, with his features clean-shaven and relaxed, Abby thought him almost stunning. It was at that second Abby was caught staring. For the first time in their association, Abby felt vulnerable.

"I just wanted to make sure you were okay," she nearly stuttered. "Do you want me to clean things up a bit?"

Paul nodded without answering and closed his eyes as he tried to dispel the lingering image of her standing there so uncertainly for the first time. He did not want to be attracted to this woman. It would be disloyal to Corrine.

He told himself he did not like fat redheads and forced himself to concentrate on Corrine's image: tall, willowy, silver-blonde hair. It was getting harder and harder to remember her smile. He had seen it so briefly.

As Abby worked around the bed, using a small brush to remove the hair, he tried to ignore her. Usually all he had to do was center his mind on the pain in his legs, but they didn't hurt so much now and that didn't work. He felt Abby lean over him, and the fragrance of her bath oil drifted to his nose.

Jasmine. Rage exploded in Paul's brain. He didn't want to smell jasmine. Corrine had always smelled of roses, and Paul wanted nothing to destroy that memory.

"What is that stuff you're wearing? The stink is enough to choke a man."

The outburst was so unexpected that Abby jumped back in surprise. To her horror, tears flooded her eyes as she realized what he had just said to her. Ian had loved the smell of her bath oil, and now her patient thought she stank.

Never would Abby have dreamt such a small thing could cause the dam to burst, but without finishing her task she ran from the room.

Her bed pillows were the recipients of Abby's tears which came in a torrent. Her eyes felt twice their regular size when she woke hours later to the sound of knocking on the door.

It was Lenore. "Abby, there's a man here. He's nearly frantic with worry. He can't find the doctor or midwife, and he's heard you were a nurse. His wife is having their first child, and he's terrified."

The nurse in Abby wanted to leave immediately, but she was here to do a job. "What about Mr. Cameron?" Abby asked. "I can't just leave."

"I'll see to him. You go and do what you can."

Abby quickly pulled herself together and rushed down the stairs. The man waiting for her was young, and he did indeed look sick with worry. He pulled her along explaining as they went, and causing Abby to nearly run to stay up with him.

— ✣ —

Paul waited all afternoon for his nurse to return. Her reaction to his comment was certainly puzzling. Red usually gave as good as she got, and he had said much worse things than not liking her perfume. He felt irritated over realizing it wasn't even true. She had smelled very nice.

As time went on, he wondered if she had quit. He would have guessed she had more mettle than that, but women were unpredictable creatures at best. Paul looked to the door in unconscious anticipation when he heard movement.

A woman walked in; it was not Red. He felt a stab of disappointment and knew it stemmed from being cheated out of picking a fight with his nurse.

"Who are you?" he asked belligerently.

Lenore had prepared herself for the worst, having stood in the kitchen many times listening to him yell at Abby. She answered calmly and hoped he wouldn't notice her shaking.

"I'm Mrs. Beckett. I brought your supper."

Paul was spoiling for a fight. "Where's the redhead? I wouldn't think your husband would appreciate having the nurse he hired run out on her job like that." Paul hoped perversely he had just gotten her in trouble.

"Oh, we didn't hire Abby. She's seeing to a delivery in town. She'll be back later," Lenore answered innocently, eyes on the tray she was straightening. She had made such an effort to have everything nice, even cutting a flower from the garden to put on his tray.

By the time she looked up, the surprise was off Paul's face. "Can I get you anything else?"

"No," Paul answered, his expression completely covering his feelings. Lenore, thinking things had gone much better than she had hoped, told him she would be back for the tray and left Paul to his supper.

The tray sat untouched for a long time. Several possibilities ran through Paul's mind as to what was going on. He finally decided it was not worth his effort to try and figure it out. He smiled cynically. He was confident of getting his answers. "Oh yes," he thought, "I'll have my answers—just as soon as I see Red."

— ✤ —

Abby placed a screaming, red newborn girl in the arms of her waiting mother and wiped some of the perspiration from her upper lip. She took a moment to bask in the sound. It never grew old. "Thank You, Lord. Thank You, Lord," Abby's heart kept repeating as she started the cleaning up in an attempt to get herself home before she collapsed.

She was both surprised and pleased to exit the small bedroom and find Ross waiting for her.

"Mother was getting worried. I've got the team out front," he said by way of explanation.

Ross could see Abby was ready to drop, so he didn't attempt any conversation even though many questions were piling up in his mind. His mother had said "Please go get Mrs. Finlayson." She hadn't said that when they had been introduced; it had just been Abigail Finlayson. Well, now was not the time to pursue the subject, but tomorrow he would pin her down.

Ross dropped Abby at the door, and she thanked him with a tired smile. Lenore was waiting up and gave her a great report on how well things had gone. Abby thanked her and briefly told of her evening as a midwife. They parted company in the kitchen where Abby, with a lamp in her hand, went in for a last check on her patient.

Abby had just set the lamp down and turned to the bed when a hand shot out and grasped her forearm with enough force to leave bruises. She gasped as she was dragged half across the bed to where Paul was leaning against the headboard. Snarling, he ordered, "Turn up the lantern."

Abby reached with her free hand to obey, her huge silver eyes nearly swallowing her face. She would never have guessed that a man bedridden for so long would be this strong. Paul waited until the light was better before he spoke again.

"Now start talking. Who are you? Who's paying you? Everything!"

Hesitating in her surprise, Abby's arm was pulled painfully until she was almost in his lap. Paul reached around the back of her head to grasp her hair. His turquoise eyes were ablaze with anger. "I said talk. *Now!*" His voice was deadly cold, and Abby started with a voice breathless and stuttering with pain.

"Your family ... sent me. Maggie, she's my aunt—your brother's nurse. I'm her niece. They heard from Mr. Beckett. I mean, Amy did—well, her father. They heard you were hurt. Your grandmother is so upset, nearly sick with worry."

Abby couldn't go on. With tears clogging her throat, she whispered pitifully, "Please, Paul, you're hurting me."

The hand holding the hair at the back of her head released slowly. He held Abby against his chest for a long moment, the anger gone from his eyes, his thoughts un-readable as he looked into the pain-filled eyes so close to his own.

Abby pushed herself from her sprawled position when his hold loosened and stood by the bed. Paul's eyes followed her movement when she unconsciously rubbed the arm he had been gripping. He was not so upset about what she had revealed as he was about the way he had treated her. Never in his life had he manhandled a woman, and he felt sick with revulsion.

How deceiving her size was! She was full-figured, but her frame was tiny. He was sure he could have snapped the bones in that arm had he twisted it. Maybe it was the confident way she stood by the bed or the fact that he was always lying down and her head was above him, but he had no idea how petite she was. Not that that was the point. His actions were reprehensible, no matter who the woman.

"I'm sorry, Mr. Cameron. It was wrong of me to let you believe Mr. Beckett was behind all of this. No one from your family came because they didn't feel they'd be welcome, and I was afraid of how you would feel when you found out, so I kept it from you."

Abby felt as though she were babbling and stopped abruptly. Paul looked at her and said nothing. He had too many questions to try and sort through tonight. Thinking she looked ready to collapse, he remembered the lateness of the hour. She had probably delivered that baby tonight, if the smears on her apron were any indication.

"We'll talk tomorrow."

Abby nodded and moved slowly toward the door.

"Red."

She turned back.

"You'll be here?" Paul suddenly thought to ask, afraid she would flee after the way he had treated her.

"I'll be here," she said softly. But as she turned away, she wished desperately she had someplace else to go.

20

Abby awoke and sat straight up in bed. She was drenched in sweat. The light told her the hour was early, and she let her body fall back on the bed. She had dreamed of Ian's dad.

He had come for her. They had camped in the woods, and he was furious. In the dream he said she had to pay, and he had tried to push her into the campfire.

Abby was afraid she would fall back asleep and dream again, so she got dressed and went down to start the coffee. As she neared the kitchen, she could smell the coffee brewing. She stopped when she noticed Paul's door was open. Voices drifted to her ears.

"I've got it on, but I haven't made it enough to know if it'll be any good."

"I don't care what it tastes like, just as long as it's hot."

"How much longer do you think you'll be laid up?"

Paul must have shrugged because Abby heard no reply. Ross went on cheerfully. "Well, I almost envy you being laid up with a beautiful nurse like Abby to wait on you."

"Listen kid," came Paul's surly reply, "it's not a bit of fun to lie here and be bossed around by that fat redhead."

Abby's hand flew to her throat in horror. It was what she deserved, standing there and listening to a private conversation. She had always been extremely sensitive about her hair and size. Phrases like, "Here comes the Fat Carrot" from the kids at school had stayed with her for years.

Her father had always told her she was pretty, and Ian had treated her as a rare jewel. But the image she had of herself was not a positive one, and hearing what Paul must have been thinking every time she was in the room was totally humiliating. Abby left the room silently, wishing she had tried to go back to sleep.

She may have felt better if she could have seen the look on Ross' face as he sat by Paul's bed. He wasn't sure why he stayed in the room, but the man fascinated him. He hadn't been the least bit polite, but he hadn't kicked him out either.

"I'd sure like to see the women where you come from if all Abby is to you is a bossy, fat redhead." Ross couldn't help but wonder if the man's eyes had been affected along with his legs.

Ross had stood across the street yesterday when Abby had gone to hire the barber. The place had nearly fallen apart. The old men on the bench out front had turned in their seats and gawked through the window like school-boys.

But Paul only grunted in answer to Ross' remark, and then asked about the coffee.

Later in the morning Abby entered the room with Paul's breakfast. He could see she was back in control, and for some reason it made him angry. Her attitude was on the cool side and, even though Paul was sure of the reason, he was irritated. She settled the tray in silence and then turned to leave.

"I said we would talk today, Red." It was an order.

Abby turned slowly and answered in a voice dripping with sarcasm. "I realize I am little more to you than a bossy, fat redhead, but I can assure you I am a person with needs of my own, and right now I'm going to eat my breakfast."

Abby had never intended to bring those words up to him, but the look of surprise on his face, brief as it was, was worth it.

Over an hour later Abby walked to the door of Paul's room feeling deceitful. She had barely touched her food. Outside the door she stopped, realizing she was acting as if faced with an inquisition. She squared her shoulders and pushed open the door.

It was obvious Paul was waiting for her. His tray was back

on the table and he was still sitting up in the bed. Wordlessly he motioned her to the rocking chair.

Abby shook her head. "I plan to change the bedding while we talk."

"The bed can wait. Have a seat."

Abby nearly balked at the command, but after a moment's hesitation she sat down, albeit reluctantly.

"How did my family know I was hurt?" Paul wasted no time in beginning his questions.

"Amy's father worked with Mr. Beckett years ago, and he remembered Amy married a Cameron. He wasn't sure you were related, but he wrote just in case."

"Who's paying you?"

"Your brother Luke gave me money for everything."

Paul's eyes were locked with Abby's, and she wished she knew his thoughts. "I want," he said slowly, "a complete accounting of every dime you've spent: your wages, clothing, train fare—everything."

Of all the things Abby had tried to prepare herself for, this wasn't one of them. In bewilderment she asked why.

"Because you're going to close my account at the bank and pay Luke every penny."

Abby's mouth nearly swung on its hinges. What in the world had made this man so bitter against a family who obviously loved him?

Abby couldn't know what being a younger brother to Luke, Mark, and Silas was all about. They never seemed to have any doubts. Luke and Silas had wanted to run the ranch from the time they were able to walk. And as a kid, Mark had been constantly on the lookout for some hurt animal to doctor. It wasn't that Paul didn't find horse breeding interesting or that he wasn't compassionate, but neither of those occupations appealed to him.

His family hadn't meant to, but they had made him feel like a failure. The only thing that had kept him going was the remembrance of a Sunday afternoon on the back porch with his brother-in-law Mac.

"I will not send money back to Luke. I don't have any idea what caused the bitterness that drives you, but your family sent me here in love, sick with worry about your plight. I will not be so cruel as to throw money back in their faces. If you want that money returned, you'll have to drag your backside out of that bed and do it yourself." Abby was on her feet by the bed, eyes brilliant with anger.

"Watch it, Red," Paul said in a deadly voice.

"My name is *Mrs.* Finlayson," she gritted out between clenched teeth.

"Well, I pity *Mr.* Finlayson. He must be crazy to be married to you."

Abby's hand cracked against his cheek. "Ian Finlayson was more man than you could ever hope to be. I'll not listen to a single word against him."

Abby swept up the tray and nearly stormed from the room, but stopped short at the door. "Let me make something clear. I'm up here as a favor to your grandmother. I suspect she doesn't realize what a coward you are, Mr. Cameron. Did you think you were the only person to ever feel pain and loss? Well, wake up and look around! Everyone hurts in some way. I'll be back at lunchtime. If you need anything before then, get it yourself." The door slammed on her last words.

21

Fingering his stinging cheek, Paul sat in stunned silence after the slamming of the door. No one had ever talked to him like that before. He was not furious, as could have been expected.

Paul shifted himself down to where he lay flat. As always, the change in position sent pains shooting through his body, but the pain was lessening some every day. His wrist was as good as new.

He was healing. He had honestly believed he was never going to walk again and planned to use that excuse to remain bitter toward God forever. But he *was* healing.

Paul lay back and let his mind get used to the idea. He fell asleep with thoughts of Corrine, wondering when, if ever, his heart would follow his legs in the healing process.

— ✧ —

Abby walked in the garden at the back of the Beckett home. The flowers were lovely and in full bloom, but she hardly noticed them. Was it wrong to speak to Paul in such a way? Maybe he had reasons to turn from his family. No, Abby couldn't believe that. Surely whatever had happened, God could take care of it.

A new thought occurred to Abby. Paul's whole family knew Christ, but maybe Paul had never made that step. Grandma Em had admitted to praying for him his whole life. At the time Abby had taken that to mean she loved him and wanted him to walk with God. But maybe he had never faced eternity and looked to the Savior.

Abby recalled her parting shot to him and felt deep shame. She was here to take care of him, and she had told him in no uncertain terms that for this morning, at least, she couldn't be bothered.

She decided right then to go back to the house and ask his forgiveness, but when she turned Ross was coming her way.

"You're a hard lady to track down," he called to her as he approached. He motioned to her when he was a few yards away. "Come over and sit down. It's too warm for work today."

Abby came forward to sit on the iron bench off the pathway. Ross joined her the minute she had adjusted her skirts.

"How's the patient?"

"Coming along, I think."

"You two sure have a hard time talking in normal tones to each other."

Abby felt a warmth creeping into her cheeks, turning them a most becoming shade. Ross was enthralled and, without thinking, bent his head. Abby whispered, "No, Ross" just before his lips touched hers.

Abby pulled away quickly as she felt Ross' arms begin to encircle her. She would have leapt from the bench, but Ross caught her hand and held it fast.

"Tell me it isn't true, Abby. Tell me you're not married. I don't think I could stand it. Tell me your name is not Mrs. Finlayson." Ross had planned to be so calm when he asked her, but when she blushed, turning her already creamy complexion rosy with embarrassment, he lost his head.

"Let go of me, Ross." Abby tried to sound reproving, but she was shaken.

"Not until you answer me. Is your name Mrs. Finlayson?"

"Yes, Ross, it is."

"But where is your husband?" Ross' look showed complete confusion. He couldn't believe any man would let this woman out of his sight.

"He's in a grave in Canada."

Ross stared at her. He was sure there was no way she was old enough to be married, let alone widowed. And then he felt young and foolish. What a protected little world he lived in! She could easily have been married and widowed. She wasn't *that* young. And it was just a way of life. If her husband had been a logger, it was practically expected that he would die young.

"Ross, I never thought you didn't understand. I probably wouldn't be here if Ian were still alive. You must be thinking I'm younger than I am."

Ross was almost afraid to ask. But even as she told him, it began to make sense. How could she be a trained nurse if she were hardly out of the schoolroom?

"I'm sorry if I caused you pain with my questions. But honestly, you don't look like a widow."

Abby did not take exception. "Ross, I loved my husband and still do. It hasn't been very long. But Ross, Ian's death was not a waste. He was a man of God, and when it was God's time he go home, not even I in my love for him would have wanted to stop him.

"I'm not worried about where he is, because we both believed in Jesus Christ, and I'm sure when I see Christ I'll see Ian again."

Ross was completely silent, his eyes telling her he was catching every word. Abby felt as if he might ask her some questions, but she was not to know on that day because Lenore was walking their way and calling to them. Abby could only pray she and Ross would get another chance to talk about Christ. After all, she had a promise to keep.

22

The morning dawned beautifully, finding Abby with wonderful peace of mind. The day before she had prayed long and hard before going in to talk with Paul, and he had been very polite. Abby had been stunned speechless when he had even apologized for his remark. The constant sparring was weighing on her, and it was a relief to have some peace.

Now she stood before the mirror and looked at her reflection. She was dressed in her best gown—the gray percale from Grandma Em. It was the first time she had worn it, for she was to attend church with the Becketts.

She worried she might be keeping everyone, and so she rushed to tell Paul he would be in the hands of Anna for the next several hours.

"Mr. Cameron," she spoke as she crossed to the bed, "I'm going to church with the Becketts. Anna, the Becketts' cook, will be right in the kitchen if you need anything." Abby hesitated and continued on almost to herself. "Well, actually I just remembered that she doesn't speak a bit of English. Maybe I shouldn't go."

"I'll be fine," Paul said gravely, almost smiling at how seriously she took her job.

Abby studied him awhile, deciding. Seconds ticked by. Paul lay quietly under her scrutiny until Abby realized what was wrong. Paul was flushed. He started when her hand came out and touched his cheek.

"You feel feverish."

"I'm fine," Paul said, thinking the scratchiness in his throat was not worth mentioning.

Abby was not to be dissuaded. Her hands came out to frame either side of his jaw, and then traveled down his throat. Paul captured her wrists in his hands.

"I am fine, Red." He enunciated each word slowly, as though speaking to a child, and called her Red in hopes of making her angry enough to leave. For some reason it made him feel terribly guilty to think of her missing church on account of him.

Abby shook her head and went for the door. "Go to church, I'm okay." This time Paul's voice was a bit croaky, and Abby whirled and came back to the bed.

"Is your throat sore?" Abby demanded.

Paul looked at her in stubborn silence. He watched her leave the room, muttering to herself all the way. "Lenore," her voice sounded out in the kitchen, and Paul knew she was telling Mrs. Beckett she would not be going to church.

"No doubt telling her I'm at death's door. You'd think I was an infant the way she behaves." But the ceiling didn't answer Paul, and he was scowling when Abby came back.

"What's that stuff?" Paul suspiciously eyed the large bottle in her hands.

"It's for colds." She began to open the bottle.

"I'm not taking that stuff." His voice was unyielding.

"Do you think your brother Mark is a good doctor?"

"What does that have to do with anything?"

"Do you?" Abby persisted.

"Yes, he's an excellent doctor. Were you planning to bring him up because I'm obviously at death's door?"

Abby ignored his sarcasm. "He gave me this for colds, which is what I suspect you're coming down with. Do you know how many people develop pneumonia when bedridden? Now you're going to take this, Paul Cameron, if I have to pour it down your throat."

It was a hollow threat, and they both knew it. She could never overpower him physically. But the stubbornness went out of him as he watched her. His voice was soft when he spoke.

"You look like a spitting red kitten when you're mad."

Abby said nothing. He was not angry or being mean, and she thought if he wanted he could use that voice to melt snow in midwinter. She hoped he wouldn't notice her hand shaking as she poured the liquid.

His look was beginning to unnerve her, and when he asked his next question she nearly spilled medicine all over the bed. "Where's your husband, Red?" His thoughts were running along those of Ross': No man would let this woman out of his sight if he could help it.

The hand holding the spoon stopped short on its path to his mouth. "He's dead." Paul's eyes narrowed, and they shared a long, mutual look. Paul knew at that moment that she was aware of his widower status. It didn't bother him—actually, it felt rather good to know someone else felt as he did.

Her words from before came back to him in full force: "Ian Finlayson *was* more man than you could ever hope to be." He had missed her usage of the past tense because of the other words. And then as she had stood by the door she had said, "Did you think you were the only person to feel pain and loss? Wake up and look around...."

Paul took the medicine without complaint. Abby, thinking it might make him sleep, went upstairs to change and give him some quiet.

23

Abby's very real fear of Paul developing pneumonia kept her near him about twice as much as before. They got along relatively well and even began to talk some.

Somehow sensing that Paul did in fact know Christ but was living in a very bitter, walled-off world, Abby prayed to be used in some way to bring him back into full fellowship with God. She knew if he was God's child, God would not give up on him. Every day she prayed for strength to treat him with Christ's love, knowing she was again striving to keep her promise.

Abby did finally make it to church with the Becketts and found herself very disappointed. Ian had had such love for his congregation. Loving your flock meant working beside them, being willing to come out of your clean church and pulpit and soil your hands alongside a neighbor who needed Christ. Abby knew that looks could be deceiving, but she wondered if the man in the pulpit that morning, droning on about the terrible state of the world, had ever worked a day in his life.

Abby smiled to herself as she realized how much living with Ian had made her think like he had.

"Want to share that smile?" The question came from Lenore as they walked behind the men.

"I was thinking of my husband."

"Can you talk about him yet?"

"It's getting easier. Ian was a pastor, so I can't attend church without seeing him in the pulpit and missing him so much it hurts."

Abby noticed absently that Lenore was slowing her step down, and when she spoke the men were quite a bit ahead of them. "Ross is a good boy, Abby. I know we spoil him, but

Sam has had to do nothing but work all his life. He never really had a childhood and time for boyish pranks. Ross will be 18 soon, and that's the time Sam always felt he would start pushing him toward some type of work. Sometimes I think Sam is more married to the mill than he is to me, he spends so much time there. It was a miracle he was even at the house when you came that first day. But for all his time there, I don't think he's set on having Ross take his place.

"I know you must think my tongue is running on both ends, but when Ross drove me to the bank yesterday we passed one of the girls Ross has been interested in for years. He didn't even look at her. Abby, I think Ross is in love with you."

Abby stopped dead in her tracks and stared at Lenore. She had wondered where this conversation had been heading, but never had she suspected this. Oh, she hadn't missed the looks Ross gave her. How could she not see the way his eyes followed her every time they were in the same room? But did Lenore think Abby was encouraging him?

"Lenore, I think Ross is a fine young man but I never . . ."

"Oh Abby, I know you haven't encouraged him. I never thought that, but Ross is vulnerable where you are concerned. For all his cocky ways, Ross is very close to us. And well, you're like a mother/lover figure all tied into one. He loves your tender ways one minute, and then the way you boss him around the next. He's also more than a little attracted to your looks. I think he's feeling things he's never felt before. I see it in his eyes and the way he can't keep them off you.

"And Abby, there is one more thing. He told me he's never heard anyone talk about God the way you do. There's no doubt in my mind my son is fascinated and, at the very least, infatuated with you."

The women had resumed their pace and the men, noticing their having dropped back, were waiting up ahead. "Thank you, Lenore, for telling me what you feel. I would never do anything to hurt Ross. I care for Ross, but my feelings for him are not serious. If his are, then he's going to be hurt no matter what. Maybe I should move Mr. Cameron. We could possibly..."

"Oh Abby, I never intended you to think such a thing. I just wanted you to be aware. I know you'll be sensitive to his feelings." They were close to the men now, and Lenore finished with a kind smile.

Abby watched husband and wife exchange a look as Lenore slipped her arm through Sam's. Lenore had obviously discussed it with her spouse in their concern for a son they loved very much. Ross saw none of the glances passed between his parents. As usual, he had eyes only for Abby.

24

The day was warm and sunny and Abby had a hard time keeping her secret while serving Paul his breakfast.

"You look rather pleased with yourself. What sinister deed are you planning against me now?"

Abby attempted an indignant look. "I can't imagine what you're talking about. And I have never been sinister!"

Paul was not the least bit fooled, but he said no more. He watched her closely. It wasn't hard to do with her cheeks glowing in good health, her complexion, peaches-and-cream. Her dress was a pale green, and Paul's eyes kept straying to her hair.

"How long is your hair?" She had checked on him in the nights with it unbound, but the lamp was always low.

She looked up in surprise, and Paul remembered she thought he didn't find her the least bit attractive. Well, she was wrong. At times he was angry with her because she was strong and healthy and Corrine was dead, but he *was* attracted to her. He had even found himself trying to talk to God about his feelings the night before.

Abby never did answer his question. She was well-experienced in ignoring questions of a personal nature from her patients.

Not until after she left did Paul realize he had not wormed out of her what mischief she had been planning. He hadn't long to wait. Half an hour later the woman he had come to know as Anna the cook came in with a smile and removed his tray. She left the door standing open as she exited and Abby came through promptly, pushing a wheeled chair.

Her smile was so triumphant that Paul laughed. His laugh had a rusty sound to it but was so beautiful that Abby felt tears sting her eyes.

"You, Mr. Cameron," she said quickly to cover her emotions, "are going to get out of that bed today." She pushed the chair close to the bed and took some clothing out of the seat. "Can you manage this or would you like some help?"

Paul took her offer of help, and within a short time was ready to be moved into the chair. It took some maneuvering, but with a lot of grunting and some pain, Paul found himself seated in the chair. The farthest he had been thus far was to the side of the bed to dangle his legs for only a few seconds. The new position caused him some dizziness, but Abby had expected this and was very close, her arms supporting him.

Paul opened his eyes to find her so close that the desire to kiss her was nearly irresistible. But he was an expert at hiding his feelings, and Abby felt in no way threatened.

"Are you okay?"

He nodded and then caught his breath when she smiled at him. Sparkling white teeth shone out at him, framed by the lovely curve of her mouth, and Paul wanted to crush her in his arms.

"Are you sure you're okay?" Abby asked again, having misinterpreted the gasp.

He was thinking he wouldn't be if she didn't put some space between them, but he refrained from commenting. Another nod was her answer, and Abby moved to steer the chair toward the door, hoping she wasn't rushing him.

"Where are we headed?" It was easier to talk with her behind him.

"You'll see," was the mysterious reply.

Paul had been wondering what the rest of the house looked like and was sure he was about to find out. Abby had other ideas, and Paul soon saw that he was being steered outside. "She has been busy," he thought when they reached the back steps that led to the garden, for Ross had rigged a type of ramp over the stairs and was waiting to help Abby with the chair and ease the ride over the bumps.

Thinking he had been set free, Paul breathed deeply of the fresh air in the garden. Ross pushed the chair out to the iron bench and parked it so it was facing where he and Abby would sit.

They talked quietly for a while, but mostly just basked in the warmth of the morning sun and enjoyed the beautiful colors of the garden. The Becketts had a gardener so everything was in perfect order. Abby wondered what that might be like—having a cook that came in every day, a gardener during the week, and once a week two women to clean things from top to bottom.

Abby hadn't had to do a bit of laundry since she arrived. When she pinned down Mr. Beckett one night about payment, he wouldn't even talk to her about it. "Grant would do the same for my family" was all he would say.

As usual, Ross hung on Abby's every word and was kind to a fault. Abby knew he wished he was older. That was unfortunate because it wouldn't have made a bit of difference. Abby believed with all her heart she would never love again.

Ross had told his father he would run some errands for him, and so he said he would have to help Paul back into the house now. The disappointment on Paul's face was so keen that Abby said she was sure she could do it on her own. Ross looked skeptical, but he had to be on his way and soon Paul and Abby were alone.

Ross couldn't have been more than two feet out of earshot when Paul said, "He's in love with you."

Abby looked away into the garden, her cheeks heating slightly. He probably thinks it's hilarious, Abby thought, that the boy is so desperate he's fallen for a fat old redhead. That this was the farthest thought from Paul's mind, Abby was not to know.

"He's young and I've never encouraged him."

"I'm sure you haven't" was Paul's surprising reply.

The birds sang and the breeze rustled some of the leaves. Abby turned to look at the man across from her. He really was incredibly handsome. His eyes were a shade of deep blue-green, clear and solemn in the sunlight. A lock of dark hair fell over his forehead, and Abby had the urge to brush it back.

The eyes and hair, combined with a perfectly shaped forehead and nose, atop a mouth that did not smile enough, and added to all of that a strong jaw and chin: In Abby's mind Paul Cameron was gorgeous. But he wasn't Ian.

She was sure if the men stood side by side Paul would be the better-looking, but he didn't look at her with eyes of love. He wasn't the man that made her heart thunder in her chest when he walked into a room. He wasn't the man of God who was a fine leader and head of their home. She liked Paul more than she had ever thought possible, but he just wasn't Ian.

"How long has he been gone?" It was as though he read her mind.

"Forever," she whispered.

"I know." Paul's reply was equally soft. "His name was Ian?"

"Ian Finlayson Jr."

"Is Ian Finlayson Sr. alive?"

Abby had dreamed again of her father-in-law just the night before, and a shiver ran over her.

Paul's hand came out to touch her arm. "What is it?"

Abby so wanted to talk with someone, and his voice was so kind, his look so tender.

"My father-in-law was devastated over Ian's death. He blames me and I left Canada because I was afraid of what he would do. I've been having dreams about him coming after me, and sometimes I feel terrified."

"Why does he blame you?"

"I led Ian to Christ shortly after we met, and he studied to be a minister after we were married. He took a church in his hometown because he was so burdened for his father's salvation. We were living with Ian's folks because we couldn't afford a place of our own. Ian's father didn't like what had become of his son, but he loved him very much and was willing to hold his peace because he could see how happy Ian and I were.

"One night a woman who attended our church came and said her son and husband were having a terrible row. She begged Ian to come. It was an accident, everyone agreed, but it didn't change the fact that Ian was dead. The son had pulled a gun and Ian was hit. I was told he didn't live longer than a few minutes."

So few words, Paul thought, so few words to describe so much pain. "Is there really a chance Ian's father would come after you?"

"I'm not sure. After the funeral he was so angry. He said he wished I were dead."

They sat in silence, and Abby couldn't believe how much better she felt. Talking to someone, having shared her burden, lifted the weight from her shoulders.

Abby wondered if Paul would ever share with her. She hoped he would feel free, but he said nothing, just looked at her with eyes of compassion and concern. What a wonderful pastor he would make, Abby thought, but she kept the thought to herself. It was nearing noon and time to head in.

25

Dear Gram,

I'm sorry I haven't written to you prior to this time, but I was not able. I am still laid up—but recovering, getting stronger each day. Mrs. Finlayson tells me she wrote you upon her arrival so you knew I was, in fact, alive. I'm sorry for your worry. I understand why you didn't write. Thank you for sensing my need for time. A letter from you would be very welcome. I cannot promise to come directly there upon recovery. I am still undecided as to my destination. Please take care. I love you Gram, Paul.

My Dearest Paul,

Thank you for your letter. I could sense it was not easy for you to write. I pray for you daily, asking for a recovery of health and spirit. I'll not press you now for how you are. Just know that I pray always.

Please tell Abby an older man was here to see her. He would not give his name, so I did not tell him of her whereabouts. I hope I did right, but he acted so aggressive, I was a little afraid for her. I so wish you were both here. It's so hard to have you down and not be by your side.

In the short time she was here, Abby became very dear to me, and this man being here made me worry for her.

I will close now and write again later. I love you, Paul. Please tell Abby of my love for her also. Gram.

— ✛ —

"Anna?"

As Paul hoped, she came to the door. "Can you please tell Red I need her."

Anna stared at him, not sure what he wanted.

"The nurse," he said slowly.

Still she stared.

"Abby."

Nothing.

"Mrs. Finlayson."

Anna's face lit with a smile, and she hustled out of the room. Paul shook his head as he adjusted himself in the chair and waited. It didn't occur to him how his summons would scare her until she rushed, wide-eyed with concern, into the room.

"Paul?" she called him without thought. "What is it? Are you in pain?"

"Slow down, Abby. I didn't mean to scare you. I just need to tell you something."

Abby took a few minutes to calm her heart and dropped heavily into the rocking chair. Paul had never asked her for anything. Lately he had been more agreeable than ever, but he had never requested anything of her, always waiting for her to offer.

"You scared me half to death."

"I'm sorry," Paul said from his place across from her.

"What did you need?" Abby's curiosity was much aroused as she stared at him.

"I heard from my grandmother. She said to tell you a man was in Baxter looking for you. He refused to give his name, so she didn't tell him where you were."

Paul did not until that moment, realize the fear under which she had been living. The color was draining away from her face and, had he not reached to block her flight, she would have run from the room.

"Abby," he spoke leaning over in his chair with his hands on the arms of the rocker, "it's alright. You don't know it was your father-in-law. And if it was, he doesn't know where you are."

"How did he know to go to Baxter?"

"Maggie lives there. Abby, you need to trust God in this as you do for everything else."

Paul didn't know who was more surprised, Abby or himself, at his statement. "I didn't tell you to scare you. But you need to be aware of what's going on. You're safe here at the Becketts. Everything is going to be fine."

And it was fine. Abby's fears were calmed as she stayed in the rocker and Paul talked to her. He was gentle and his wonderful voice and convincing manner soothed her. She wouldn't have been surprised if he asked her to pray with him, so tender and almost loving was his manner.

Near the time for Abby to see to supper, she said gently and in complete ignorance, "Your voice and manner are so comforting, Paul. You would make a wonderful pastor."

The look that came over his face was nearly frightening. Abby watched pain, anger, frustration, and finally a wall being erected in front of whatever he was feeling—and suddenly she knew.

"Tell me, Paul, that what I'm thinking is wrong. Tell me you were not a pastor and in bitterness you walked away from it." Abby's voice pleaded with him to deny it.

His face was angry, shuttered, and she knew she had guessed rightly. Abby jumped to her feet.

"How could you? How could you walk away from such a calling? To be used of God to teach the Word and tell people of His Son, and then just walk away from it all! What's become of your church? Did you just leave without notice?"

"I couldn't—wouldn't—go on preaching about a God who doesn't answer prayer," he gritted out in anger.

"Not answer your prayers?"

"He let my wife die."

Abby stared at him aghast. Her voice was heavy with scorn when she went on. "So God's plan didn't fit in with the high and mighty plans of Paul Cameron! Paul asks and Paul gets! Well, let me tell you something, Mr. Cameron: God answered your prayer alright and the answer was *no*. You asked God to spare Corrine and He said *no*. Where I come from, a "no" answer is still an answer."

Abby was out of breath from her speech but not finished. "When I think of Ian's zeal for God and his hunger to spread the Word and no longer alive to share it, and you still here obviously gifted to such a calling but unwilling, I can't," Abby's voice broke, "I can hardly stand to look at you." Abby's actions were as good as her words. She lifted her skirts and fled.

26

Abby was feeling desperate for some time away from her job. She had taken care of Paul's needs throughout supper and early evening, and it had been miserable for both of them. The anger and words between them were like an unscalable wall, and all their past disputes were made to look like child's play in the face of it.

Patient and nurse tried not to look at each other. When their eyes did meet, hers were shuttered, and Paul's remote. Abby knew she had to get away, if for no more than a few hours.

"Lenore," Abby approached her hostess before bed, "would it be a terrible inconvenience if I left the house for a while tomorrow?"

"Why no, Abby." She looked surprised, and Abby was sure she had misunderstood.

"It would mean your taking care of Paul. If you've got plans, I'll understand."

"You don't need to ask twice Abby," Mr. Beckett broke in. "I suspect Lenore has always wished she was a nurse, so being offered the chance to care for your patient is enough to make her day."

Sam smiled at Lenore, and she grinned at him almost shyly. Abby knew they had a special relationship.

"Actually, I don't know why we didn't offer first," Sam went on. "I'm sure no one expects you to work every day."

"Who should work every day?" Ross wanted to know as he sauntered into the room.

"Abby is taking the day off tomorrow," Ross' father informed him, looking pointedly at the hat still atop his son's head. Ross whipped the hat off and sent it sailing toward a chair, making his mother's eyes roll with long-suffering.

"Where are you going?" Ross asked Abby as he took a seat, not even glancing to see if his hat made it onto the chair.

"Probably just for a walk around town."

"I'm free tomorrow, and I could take you out for a drive in the buggy. We could pack a picnic and make a day of it."

Abby hesitated, sure that such a day would lead Ross to believe there could be a more serious relationship between them. She was also very aware of Sam and Lenore's eyes on her.

"Just as friends," Ross said quietly but loud enough for his parents to hear. Abby smiled at him in relief; he had understood her hesitation. She knew well that a person couldn't just decide not to care for someone, but Ross' words told her he understood where their relationship stood.

Plans were made for the next day before Abby retired for the night. Abby would sleep as late as she wanted, and they would leave with a basket of food when she arose.

Even as she drifted off to sleep, her heart still angry at what she had learned about Paul, she felt deep compassion over his bedridden state and then thought that his body was healthy compared to the malady of bitterness in his heart.

27

Abby did not sleep well in the night, so the sun was moving high in the sky by the time she and Ross set out.

"I had planned to pack the lunch for us. I feel badly that Anna had to do it."

"I don't think she minded. She likes you, and of course she adores me." Ross winked at Abby, and she laughed at his audacity.

Driving around the streets of town, Ross pointed out sights of interest. There was a mansion in town, and he drove by slowly to let Abby look her fill.

They passed timber companies, the boardinghouse, a hotel, and numerous saloons. Abby looked with interest at everything and listened attentively to Ross' running commentary.

The buggy and horse were headed out of town after their tour, and Ross took Abby to a peaceful spot along the Namekagen River that the town had grown up around.

They withdrew from the buggy with a blanket and the basket and were soon seated along the banks of the river. The sun was hot overhead and the day promising.

Abby had not eaten and planned to dig right into the basket. Ross, at the age of constant hunger, gave her no argument. As with all the meals at the Beckett home, Anna did not disappoint them. Abby pulled out from the basket: chicken, muffins, a tin of nuts, boiled eggs, cheese, crackers, tomato slices, and a layer cake, along with jugs of cold water and apple cider.

Abby had everything set out when Ross asked, "Why couldn't you have come into town and fallen in love with me the first time we met?" His tone was light, but Abby caught the underlying, very real desire.

She looked across the food-strewn blanket and into his eyes. "It's not that you would be impossible to love—"

"But I'm too young, right?"

"I wasn't going to say that. It's just that I've already given my heart, and even though Ian isn't here to hold it, I still take that commitment seriously."

"I think Ian was a lucky guy."

"I don't know about luck, Ross, but Ian and I were very blessed to be given each other."

Very blessed, Ross thought, she's always saying things like that. "Can I ask you something?"

"Sure."

"It might make you mad."

Abby looked surprised but said nothing, so Ross went on. "I heard you praying one day in your room. I know I shouldn't have listened, but when I heard you talking I wanted to know who was in there with you and well, I guess I just stood in the hall and eavesdropped."

Feeling embarrassed after his admission, Ross saw that Abby didn't look angry, and he desperately wanted to ask her about it. "Abby, do you really believe God can hear you? I mean all those things you said to Him about taking care of your family and healing Mr. Cameron. Do you really think God can do all of that?"

Abby was quiet for a few minutes, and Ross wondered what she was thinking. He would have been surprised to find out she was praying.

"Ross, I'm glad you felt you could ask me," she finally began in a gentle voice. "I'm not ashamed of my belief in God, so I'm not upset that you heard me pray. When I was a little girl, my grandmother died. I cried and cried for days, but my grandfather never shed a tear.

"It took me some time, but I finally asked him why. He told me that he and my grandmother had grown up together and one day a traveling preacher came to town. The man said that Jesus Christ was God's Son and that He had died on the cross for sinners. Well, my grandpa said he knew he was a sinner and needed a Savior and that day he believed on Jesus Christ. He said grandma believed that day too, and he knew she was with Christ and that's why he didn't cry. He was going to see her again.

"He asked me that day if I had ever made that decision, and I had to say no. He wanted me to pray with him right then and tell God of my sin and believe He died for me, but I said no. A few years later my grandfather lay on his death-bed and I went in to be near him. There was no fear on his face because he knew where he was going. Jesus was his Savior and grandpa was going to be with Him and see grandma again.

"Before my grandfather died that day, I knelt by his bed and with his hand holding mine I told God of my need for a Savior. The Bible says to 'believe on the Lord Jesus Christ and thou shalt be saved.' Well, Ross, I did believe and I've never been the same.

"The God of all creation lives inside of me, and without Him I am nothing. I grew up in a home where prayer—talking with God—was a daily occurrence. Jesus Christ is my best friend, and when I pray, I pray believing He loves me and His will for me will be perfect. It was hard to lose Ian, but I know it was God's will and that I'll see Ian again."

Abby was sure she had rambled on too long. It was Ian who was the preacher, not she; Ross would be thoroughly confused.

"How can I know your God?"

Abby couldn't believe her ears. She had been so absorbed in the recounting of her story, she had missed the look on Ross' face. It was a look of wonder and searching. Abby wanted to throw her arms around him.

With a trembling voice, Abby answered. "John 3:16 says 'For God so loved the world, that he gave his only begotten Son, that whosoever believeth in him should not perish, but have everlasting life.' All you need to do is believe in Him, that He can save you from sin, and He does all the rest. He receives you as His child, and you're His for all eternity."

Ross nodded slowly, and Abby felt her heart pound as she asked, "Ross, would you like me to pray with you?"

"No," he said softly, "I think I understand."

Abby watched quietly, tears swimming in her eyes, as Ross bowed his head before God. She prayed also. When he raised his head, Abby was working hard at removing the evidence of tears from her face.

"I don't feel any different."

"Do you believe you are a sinner, Ross, and do you believe Christ died for that sin?"

He nodded and Abby said, "Then you are now a child of God. You don't need to feel any different. God promised in the Bible that those who believe on Him would be saved, and He never breaks a promise."

"I want to know more about the Bible," Ross stated simply, and Abby laughed in delight. "Your wanting to read God's Word is one of the signs that there has been a change."

Ross smiled at her and laughed too. He thought she had come here to be his wife, but now he could see her purpose had been altogether different. Ross' smile nearly stretched off his face when words came to his heart that he had never said before: "Thank You, God."

28

Ross and Abby spent most of the day on the bank of the river. He asked questions of her and Abby did her best to answer them. Time and again she wished for her Bible.

"Do you get everything you pray for?"

"No, it really isn't like that. I try not to treat God like a magical being who I call upon when I need help. When I pray, I claim verses of Scripture. Like God's promise that He died for all, well, I prayed then for you and your folks that maybe something I could do or say would help you turn to Christ."

Abby hoped she was making sense. Rarely did anyone question her with the newborn hunger that Ross displayed, and Abby felt all she could do was tell him of her own personal experiences.

Feeling more and more excited with each passing hour, Ross remembered as Abby talked where he had put his Bible. The second he got home he planned to open it.

Abby would cry sometimes in telling of her background, and Ross' heart felt so tender toward her he had to fight the urge to take her in his arms. He could easily see what a wonderful pastor's wife she must have been.

"Abby, do you think you could ever feel any different about me, now that I'm a Christian?"

"I don't think you understand, Ross, how recently it happened or how sudden. Not too many weeks ago I was a happily married woman, praying for my husband as he went to help someone from our church. In less than an hour a man was at our door telling me Ian was dead. I still felt like a bride, and suddenly I was a widow.

"I'm flattered that you care for me, but I'm not the woman for you, Ross. If God does have a wife in your future,

107

He'll show you, but I think I can speak with surety, Ross—I'm not that woman."

They ate in silence and Ross was surprised to find he was not devastated. He had asked the question with little hope, but she was so special he couldn't resist checking with her one more time. He said a brief prayer thanking God for Abby and this chance to talk with her. He couldn't believe how much better he felt after he had uttered the simple words to his newfound heavenly Father.

Back on the first floor of the Beckett home, Paul was also talking with his heavenly Father, but his words weren't those of thanksgiving. Mrs. Beckett had been in for both breakfast and lunch, along with occasional checks on him—all of which was enough to tell him his nurse was gone.

"Why did you bring her here? Why?" Paul wanted to shout the words, but they were whispered to God. He had been building such a strong, impenetrable wall against his emotions, and then she came along and began to scale that wall. Her words to him yesterday would have slid off him like logs on a mountain if they had been said when he first arrived.

But no, he had begun to soften. She was doing it to him with her kindness and loving care. Her soft words and gentle touch as she saw to his needs would have been enough. But when she confided that her husband was dead, causing pain to cloud those beautiful gray eyes, and he knew she was in the same state as he, it had been more than he could take.

For the first time since Corrine's death, Paul felt shame. "Did you think you were the only one to have pain?" Her words sent agony through him. He didn't want to meet someone who was able to go on in spite of her pain. He wanted to be strong without God. But he wasn't strong—

not in the least. Each day his spirit grew weaker and weaker, and his need to turn to God pressed in with more insistency.

Paul threw his arm over eyes that had begun to fill with tears, the pain in his troubled, rebellious heart nearly splitting him in two. "Please, help me, God," Paul cried as his body began to shake with sobs, the first he had shed since Corrine's death. "Please help me come back to You."

A few hours later when Lenore went in to give Paul his supper, she found him asleep. The evidence of tears on his face and lashes nearly started her own. She left the tray by his bed and went as soundlessly as she could from the room, wishing as she did that Abby was there. She doubted that Paul Cameron would ever admit it, but he needed Abigail Finlayson.

It was a tired Abigail Finlayson climbing the stairs toward her bedroom that night. She wondered if Ian had felt this weary after a day of counseling someone.

It took her a little while in her weary state to ready for bed. While she did so, she couldn't help but wonder how Lenore had done with Paul.

Renewed anger surged within her as their conversation of the day before came to mind. *How* could he leave his church? The thought was incomprehensible to her. What a waste! What a foolish waste! How in the world was she going to go on taking care of him when the very thought of him made her blood boil?

Anger moved her a little faster toward bed, and soon she was beneath the covers. Sleep however, did not immediately come. With her anger stirred, she didn't feel a bit tired.

"Turning your back on your family," her mind railed at him. "All the love they have for you, and you treat them as though they were responsible for your wife's death. Foolishness, absolute foolishness!"

"Paul's sin of bitterness is against God, Abby, not yourself. *You* have no right to be angry. God has the right, but He's not angry. He still loves Paul and waits patiently for him to return to his heavenly Father."

Abby didn't know where the words came from, but they drained the anger from her like water through a sieve. Tears clogged her throat when she thought of herself trying to deal with Ian's death on her own. She would never have made it. But that was exactly what Paul had chosen to do. Rather than put his hand in God's as he walked the path of hurt and loss, he had chosen to go alone.

"Oh God," Abby cried, "please help him. I'm sorry I was so insensitive to his plight. Please cover him with Your love. Show him that without You he'll never get over the hurt. He'll never be used of You as he was meant to be."

Abby cried long and hard then, her heart and mind unable to form sentences. She cried for Paul and for herself. And she cried tears of joy for Ross' newfound faith.

Her tears were healing ones and, though she did not know it, her prayers were desperately needed for the man downstairs who was wide awake and starting down the road to a recovered heart.

29

Surprised to enter Paul's room the next morning and find him still asleep, Abby felt a bit of concern. He was usually wide awake and starving.

"Mr. Cameron," she called softly, a little afraid of having him take her head off. "Mr. Cameron," she called again, this time reaching out to touch his shoulder.

Paul reached up with both hands and scrubbed furiously at his face in an effort to get his eyes open. Abby thought he looked exhausted when his eyes met hers.

"I wasn't expecting to find you asleep. I thought maybe you were ill."

"No, just tired," Paul answered, thinking as he did that he had been sure he was never going to see this woman again and if by chance he did see her, she certainly wouldn't be the kind, gentle person standing by his bed.

Abby's surprise was no less than Paul's. The eyes looking at her were tired, but there was no anger or remoteness like the last time she had seen him.

"Would you like to sleep some more, or do you want breakfast?"

What I want, he thought, is for you to sit down and talk to me and be near me the rest of the day. But all he said was, "I'll eat, thanks."

He watched her leave with regret and praise. Praise because she wasn't gone as he had thought. And regret because he wanted her to stay so he could share what had gone on in the last day.

He wanted to tell her of his night of confession and surrender, his night of tears and the giving over of his will to God. And then God showering him with verses and hymns from his memory, telling of God's love, patience, long-suffering, power, might, strength, compassion. The list was endless!

Paul's heart overflowed again in the morning light as he thanked God for drawing his attention back to Him. Every day the Spirit of God had beckoned to him with open arms, and Paul's heart was full of praise that He hadn't given up on him.

Abby returned with the tray and suddenly Paul felt ravenous. She looked at him strangely when he thanked her, and he felt shame at the way he had treated her.

After breakfast Abby held the mirror while Paul shaved. She nearly dropped it when, wiping his face, he handed her the towel and said, "Abby, can you get me my Bible?"

Staring into his eyes in astonishment, Abby waited for the cynical gleam to appear, but he met her look squarely without a trace of the barrier he usually kept between them.

"You want me to get your Bible?" Abby's voice shook and her eyes continued to search his. What she saw made her lower lip tremble and her eyes fill with tears. He was so vulnerable at that moment.

"Hey, Red," he said softly, his voice like a caress, "you didn't really think God would give up on me, did you?"

It was too much for Abby. She dropped the mirror onto the bed and buried her face in Paul's wet towel. Paul felt helpless as he watched her cry. Were he able to get out of the bed, he would have taken her into his arms.

The thought of holding her made him want to have her closer. He reached and caught hold of the towel she was adding wetness to and pulled her to the head of the bed.

As Abigail began to contain herself, Paul took the towel and wiped her face. He held one of her hands and tenderly dried her wet cheeks. When she hiccuped, Paul laughed.

"Your nose is red. If I didn't know better, I'd say you'd been drinking."

Abby smiled a very watery smile and said, "You took me so totally by surprise. I mean—"

"I know what you mean, no need to explain." He gently squeezed her hand and then released it.

They looked at one another in silence. "I prayed for you last night, confessed my anger. I gave it and you over to God," Abby said softly.

"I did some confessing of my own and God was waiting, Abby, with arms outstretched, to draw me back into His fellowship."

"If you ever want to tell me all about it, I'll listen."

"Thanks."

Abby moved to the wardrobe and retrieved Paul's Bible from the shelf where she had placed it after finding it in his things. He thanked her when she handed it to him.

"Where were you yesterday?"

Pausing in the gathering of shaving gear, Abby replied, "Ross and I went for a drive and a picnic."

"Are things getting a little serious between you?"

"No, it's nothing like that, but it was an exciting day. Ross trusted in Christ. He's a new Christian."

"That's great," Paul exclaimed, his face alive with excitement. Sitting up straighter in bed, he eagerly demanded, "Tell me everything!"

Abby described Ross' conversion and Paul was thrilled. When she finished, Paul asked, "Will you tell Ross I'd like to talk with him sometime?"

"Sure," Abby said as she moved to the door.

"By the way, Abby," Paul's voice stopped her, "thank you for being here when both Ross and I needed you."

Abby smiled at him and didn't answer, but she went out thinking, "I had to be here, Paul. I have a promise to keep."

30

Ross was perched on a kitchen chair and Abby sat in the rocker. They were in Paul's room, and the three of them had their Bibles opened to Romans 12.

Paul read verses 1 and 2: "I beseech you therefore, brethren, by the mercies of God, that ye present your bodies a living sacrifice, holy, acceptable unto God, which is your reasonable service. And be not conformed to this world, but be ye transformed by the renewing of your mind, that ye may prove what is that good, and acceptable, and perfect, will of God."

"What's a living sacrifice?" Ross wanted to know.

"It's when we give our bodies and lives to Christ."

Ross looked a little confused, so Paul went on. "You see, Ross, God gives us choices. He doesn't take our free will—He *asks* us to give Him our bodies for His work and service."

"And if someone doesn't choose to serve Him?" Ross wanted to know.

"Like I said, Ross, the choice is our own, but that person will be miserable, I can assure you," Paul answered him soberly.

"I had dedicated my life to God, but then in my bitterness I walked away from that commitment. I was about as far as I could get from presenting my body as a living sacrifice.

"But it doesn't have to be as drastic a move as mine was. I know Christians—people who claim to have trusted Christ and attend church regularly—that don't put Christ first. God, for some of them, is just a Sunday duty. They are not praying and studying His Word. The people they work with or live with don't even know of their faith because it's not evident in their lives.

"Abby is a perfect example of the way God wants it to be. You saw a difference in her because she has given her life over to God."

Abby felt humbled at Paul's words and added, "You can't lose your salvation, Ross. Never think that."

"Abby's right, Ross. Nothing can separate us from our Savior. Nothing. Not even ourselves in our willfulness. But the Scriptures also say that in Christ we are new. It should be our desire to serve Him, if there's really been a change."

It was the second time the three of them had met together to study God's Word. On the same day Paul asked Abby for a Bible, she also told Ross that Paul wanted to see him.

Asking humbly for Ross' forgiveness for the way he had acted, Paul told him a little of his situation in Bayfield and about losing Corrine. Ross had been sympathetic and was fascinated with Paul being a pastor. When Paul asked Ross about studying the Bible together, the younger man nearly shouted with excitement.

Abby considered it a privilege when Paul asked her to join them, but she also told Ross the first time they studied that should he ever want to meet with Paul on his own, he had only to tell her.

Now, as they finished up for the day and Paul closed in prayer, Abby began to hope she would always be included. Paul had a wonderful grasp of the Scriptures, and Abby knew she could listen to him all day. It was also obvious when Paul prayed that he and God were not strangers.

The next few days Paul, Abby, and Ross sat in the garden for their Bible study and prayer. One day after the study concluded Ross maneuvered Paul's chair back into the house and went to see his dad.

Paul had hoped for a few minutes alone with Abby. He watched her straighten the bed, pick up the room, and open a window before he spoke.

"Do you have a minute, Abby? I have something I'd like you to read."

"Sure," Abby answered as she came to stand expectantly by the bed.

"I've written to the church in Bayfield. I wondered if you would read this and tell me what you think."

Abby sat in the rocker with the letter Paul had given her, while Paul lay back with closed eyes, wanting to give her some time to read.

"Dear Lloyd," it began, "I'm writing this letter to you because of the friendship and support you offered while I was serving as your pastor and living in your home. I ask you from the bottom of my heart and in Christ's love to forgive me for the way I treated you, May, and the congregation, and I hope you will share this letter with them.

"I believed then with all my heart that if my faith had been strong enough, God would have spared Corrine. It never really occurred to me that she would die. I see now that my faith was immature. It was my will that Corrine live, not God's. The pain she endured her whole life is over now, and she is in His arms.

"The time I have been gone has been a painful one. I have suffered much, both spiritually and physically, but am on the road to recovery. I am currently in Hayward laid up with two broken legs. There is so much more I want to say, but I want to be there in person.

"As soon as I'm able to travel, I'll be coming to see all of you and beg your forgiveness for deserting you. I'm praying for you every day and hope I can be there soon. Paul Cameron."

Paul opened his eyes when he heard Abby move by the bed. Her eyes were brilliant with unshed tears, and she reached to take his hand. Without uttering a single word, she gave him comfort.

It was enough for Paul, and he began to talk. "Corrine was so sick. I'm not sure she really knew how bad it was. I certainly didn't. We knew each other such a short time, and I fell so deeply in love with her. We were married in her room because she was too sick to move out of her bed. She never did get out of that bed."

There were tears in Paul's eyes now, and Abby's began to flow. Her heart broke for this man. To love and be married but never share a bed must have been almost more than he could bear. It was painful to lay in bed at night and wish that Ian's arms were around her, but at least she had that memory.

"I'm sorry, Paul, so sorry that you had to watch her die." Abby spoke the words with deepest compassion, and Paul felt comforted by her presence as well as her words. Her next words surprised him.

"Your letter to the folks in Bayfield is wonderful. It's obvious you love them. When you're ready to go, if you want, I'll go with you."

Paul couldn't know in his own surprise that Abby was equally amazed. She never planned to make any such offer, but the words just came out. She knew if he asked her she would go.

What else was God going to ask her to do? First she traveled up here unescorted, and now she offered to travel alone with a man who was not her husband. She wasn't sure she could do that.

Abby left Paul's room with her heart in a quandary. She fretted about the future all the way to her room. Then she remembered the verses she had read with Paul and Ross a few days earlier: "Present your bodies a living sacrifice." Abby had made this commitment years ago and worked daily at living as that sacrifice. Not once in all those years had God let her down. Abby was certain then if Paul asked her to go to Bayfield, she would trust God and go. Her Savior was taking care of her, and knowing this she could leave it in His hands.

31

"But Ross, you've gone to church for years, and of course you believe in God. I'm not sure what you're trying to tell us." Lenore looked at her son with honest confusion.

"This is different, Mom, and I'm not doing a very good job explaining it."

"Ross, are you trying to tell us you want to be a preacher?" The question came from his father, his face serious.

"No, that's just it. Even though I feel closer to God than I ever have before—I mean I know He's going to stay with me—well, even though I feel that way, I don't think I'm supposed to be a pastor. The truth is, I want to be a lawyer. In fact, I've never been so sure of anything."

Lenore was still looking at Ross as though she had missed something, but his father was delighted.

"This is great. It was never my plan for you to take over the mill unless, of course, you wanted it, but well...a lawyer...that's great. You'd be a fine lawyer. What are your plans?"

"I'm not sure yet. The whole idea is still pretty new. But I did want to let you know what I was thinking."

Ross and his parents talked some more, and he felt great about having told them of his faith in Christ. He also was terribly excited about a possible career in law. It had long been a thought playing around in the back of his mind, and suddenly it was as though God was saying "yes."

He knew as he left his parents to see if Paul was awake that his mother had not been comfortable about something. He hoped she would come to him when she was ready.

Ross found Paul getting ready to stand with the help of a cane by the side of the bed.

"Steady," Ross said as he shut the door and moved

quickly to his aid. "I thought you were going to wait for me to help you each day."

"I was, but I'm afraid I can't keep this cane hidden from Abby much longer, and I want to get steady on my feet before she catches me."

"You sound like a kid caught with cookie crumbs on his face."

"And you sound like you've never had Abby get after you for disobeying an order. Makes me tremble just to think of it."

Ross laughed and Paul asked, "How did things go with your parents? I was praying for all of you."

"Thanks. They loved the idea of me becoming a lawyer, but I'm not sure they understood about my faith in God."

"There are verses in 1 Peter chapter 3, Ross, that tell the wives of unsaved husbands to witness with the changes in their lives, not with words. I think they're good verses for everyone. At times our sinful actions are so loud people can't hear what we are saying about God."

Paul felt a few moments of deep regret at how "loud" his actions had been over the last few months. He had talked with Mr. and Mrs. Beckett a few days ago in an attempt to apologize for his actions in their home. They had been polite, but there was no way of knowing what they had really been thinking when he told them he was a backslidden pastor. He hoped that in the short time he had left here they would see a difference. The cane sure didn't help. He wouldn't be hobbling along with it and needing Ross' help if he'd kept his eyes on Christ. But it was over, and carrying the guilt around would only hinder his growth.

"I think that's enough for right now, Ross." Paul was out of breath and struggled to get the words out. He dropped heavily onto the edge of the bed.

"Thanks."

"Are you okay, Paul?"

"Yeah, I just feel like an old man."

"How old are you, anyhow?"

"Twenty-six."

Ross gave an exaggerated whistle. "You *are* an old man!"

Paul took a playful swing at him with the cane, and Ross grabbed it and tucked it under the bed—all of which happened none-too-soon as Abby picked that moment to join them.

Abby looked carefully at Paul and Ross. Everything appeared to be in order. Ross was in the rocking chair—a place he had sprung to when he heard the door open, and Paul was against the headboard where he had scooted himself as Ross had made for the chair. Oh yes, everything looked normal—too normal.

"Is there anything anyone would like to tell me?" Abby inquired solicitously.

"You look very pretty today, Abby," Ross said with an innocent smile.

Abby's eyes narrowed reprovingly at Ross for deliberately misunderstanding her question before swinging to Paul who was rubbing his upper lip in a suspicious manner. Suddenly Abby felt very self-conscious and wondered if she was the target of a private joke.

"Well," Abby said too brightly, "if you don't need anything, I'll just get out of your way."

"Get her back in here, Ross," Paul ordered as she sailed out the door. He was coming to know Abby like the back of his hand, and he easily read the vulnerable look on her face, even from across the room.

Within seconds Ross led Abby back into the room. Sensing immediately that his presence was not needed, he left Abby and Paul alone.

"Ross said you needed something."

Paul only stared at her wondering what he was going to do. She was under his skin in a way he never thought possible. Believing himself to still be in love with Corrine, why did he think about Abby most of the time? Why did his heart beat faster and his day seem brighter when she came into the room?

"Paul?"

"I asked Ross to bring you back because I think you believed we were having some joke at your expense." He was being up front with her.

"I could tell I came in at a bad time. How did you know what I was thinking?"

"Oh, Red," Paul laughed softly in the way that always made Abby think of being held by him. "You are as easy to read as the pages of a book."

"I am not!" Abby said, but her voice lacked all conviction. Looking for something to do with her hands, she straightened the bed and rattled on about the first thing that came to her mind.

"I don't think you are concentrating on getting out of this bed, Paul Cameron. You know you can't lay here forever. We've got to get you back on your feet. I think you'll be ready maybe as early as next week to try a few steps."

Abby stopped when her jaw was cupped in one of his long-fingered hands. He spoke with eyes looking directly into hers.

"Don't ever pretend with me, Red. No one was laughing at you, and that's a promise. And if I could get up and walk right now, well, let's just say I'm not sure if either one of us is ready for that."

There was no mistaking his meaning as he held her face close to his own. She would be lying to herself if she said she had never thought of their situation—their dual need for companionship and love. But he was right—she was not ready.

She had to get out of the room. She was going to get kissed if she didn't. In an effort to escape the draw of his beautiful blue eyes, Abby closed her own. She felt Paul's hand leave her face, his fingers sliding gently along her jaw as contact was broken.

"If you need something, Paul, send Anna," Abby spoke without once raising her eyes to his and left the room.

32

The letter Paul received from Grandma Em was brief. She said she would write again later, but she felt it important to reply right away, and she had been too emotional to write more.

Paul had shared with Abby and Ross during Bible study, and Abby couldn't believe how pleased Paul was. It crossed her mind that there was something more to his happiness, but she pushed the thought aside.

Of course, dispensing with thoughts of Paul was getting harder and harder all the time. She didn't feel unfaithful to Ian, but neither did she take herself too seriously. She still loved Ian and was sure she always would. But she was also beginning to realize that God probably did have another husband somewhere for her.

Unbidden, Paul's face appeared in her mind, and Abby knew why. Abby was still thinking about the fact that he had nearly kissed her. She knew it wasn't too significant—after all it was only natural after weeks of close contact that certain emotions would come to the surface. But the whole conversation and Paul's hand touching her face preyed on her mind.

It wasn't that Abby thought herself irresistible—in fact, quite the opposite. But Paul did possess a very tender nature that really only surfaced after he "got right" with God. He probably felt some guilt about the way he had treated her and was just being extra-kind to her.

Abby went to the mirror and then wished she hadn't. To her, the freckles on her nose stood out like stars. And her hair! The humidity made it a frizzy mess! It certainly wasn't any wonder that Paul Cameron didn't find her attractive.

"I'm too self-absorbed," she told herself in an effort to take her mind off her looks. But even though she prayed all the way down the stairs, thanking God that she was alive and healthy, she was nearly depressed by the time she got to the kitchen to prepare Paul's lunch.

For the first time she was glad that Anna spoke only Norwegian. Abby was in real need of peace and quiet. When she heard Paul's door open, she figured Ross was on his way out.

"Your timing is good, Ross. I'm just about to carry this tray to Mr. Cameron." Abby turned then and moved to the door. What she saw would have caused her to drop the tray if Paul's hand had not shot out to catch it.

He was standing! Paul was standing! He stood in the doorway and filled the frame. She realized in the instant how much she cared for him. Abby should have been thrilled he was able to get out of the bed, but she wasn't. It was over. He didn't need her anymore.

"Sit down, Abby," Paul ordered her.

"Why?"

"Because you've gone white as a sheet," Paul said with concern.

Anna had come forward to rescue the tray, and Abby felt Paul's hand on her arm leading her to the table.

"You scared me," she said weakly.

"I'm sorry. It was meant to be a surprise, not a scare."

Abby gaped at him. He had taken a chair beside her, and she noticed for the first time the dark wood cane he had leaned against the table.

"It's good to see you out of that bed," she said honestly. "I take it that this is what has been going on between you and Ross when I wasn't looking?"

"Guilty as charged," he replied and held up his hands.

Full of concern, Abby asked, "Are you sure you're not rushing this? Maybe you should check with the doctor." The nurse in her was back in control of herself and the situation.

"I'm taking it very slowly."

Abby took him at his word. They sat together at the kitchen table and ate lunch. Both were subdued, and Abby wondered what Paul was thinking.

Paul was so filled with praise that he was once again walking that his mind wouldn't focus on any one thing. He was out of bed, and the woman he was coming to deeply care for—if not already love—was near. All of this was more than Paul ever could have hoped for.

He knew that very soon it would be time to go to Bayfield. He knew the trip would not be without its pain, but he was going to face all of it with Jesus Christ by his side, and in that he knew peace.

33

It was a treat for everyone to be at the Beckett supper table that evening. Paul had come out a few times in his wheeled chair to eat with them, but knowing he had come on his own two legs was extra-special.

Abby had had a good afternoon. Immediately following lunch she had gone to her room to pray. She had poured her heart out to the Lord—her feelings toward Paul, the deep hurt within her at having to face life without Ian, the fear of her father-in-law, the unaccepting attitude about herself that she knew hindered her growth in the Lord. Everything.

As she had known He would, God gave her peace. She read in Matthew 6 about God's special care for His own. She was not to be worried about tomorrow because God was in control. The last two verses, 33 and 34, were just what Abby needed:

> But seek ye first the kingdom of God, and his righteousness; and all these things shall be added unto you. Take therefore no thought for the morrow, for the morrow shall take thought for the things of itself.

Abby wondered as she readied for supper if maybe it wasn't time to go home. She really had no other place to go right now. Even if her father-in-law did go there to find her, she would see him eventually—of that she was sure. But to fear him was not to trust God, and Abby wanted that above all else: to daily place her life in His care.

Conversation around the table was light. Ross had a friend over named Dave, and Abby sat across from him with Paul on her left. Lenore was at one end of the table and Mr.

Beckett at the other end to Abby's right. Paul, Ross, Dave, and Lenore were in conversation when Mr. Beckett sent a question to Abby.

"Well, Abigail, does it feel good to get your patient on his feet?"

"Yes, it does," she said with a smile.

"What are your plans now? Where will you go when it's time to leave here?"

"I've been thinking about that, Mr. Beckett, and I've decided to go see my parents in Michigan. Maybe I'll look for work over there. I'm not sure of anything beyond that." When Abby finished talking, she realized she had the attention of the entire table. Not that she minded—she wasn't ashamed of having to support herself. It never even occurred to her to live with her parents. As a nurse she could get work in many places. To Abby, her ability to nurse was just another way of God taking care of her. Both her father and brother were doctors. Maybe one of them could use her help right now.

After supper the young people made their way out to the garden. The evening was warm and inviting. Ross and Dave moved away and Abby watched them, wondering if maybe Ross was telling Dave of his conversion. She looked away from them to find Paul watching her.

"I must say, Abby, I'm a little disappointed. You didn't strike me as a person who reneged on her words."

"I don't know what you're talking about."

"I'm talking about your plans to go to Michigan after you told me you'd go to Bayfield with me. Or maybe I misunderstood you and that isn't what you said at all."

"No, I mean, that's what I said. But you never said anything, so I assumed you didn't want me to go."

In Paul's mind the whole thing had been completely settled. She had offered and he had thanked her, and as far as he was concerned she was going. But then she didn't know how much he wanted—no, *needed*—her with him.

"I want you to go." The words were said easily, without force or as an order, but there was an intensity in Paul's eyes that Abby had never seen before.

"When do you want to leave?"

"I think the end of the week, if that's good for you. I was also thinking of asking Ross."

"Oh, Mr. Cameron, that's a wonderful idea."

"I wish you'd make up your mind as to what you're going to call me."

Abby blushed to the roots of her hair. She had really hoped the times she had slipped and called him Paul had gone unnoticed.

"I, well, I mean, I never meant to call you. I mean, I think it's presumptuous and I'm sorry."

Paul said nothing, just watched her until she ran out of words and stood before him in acute embarrassment.

"I'd like you to call me Paul. After all, you're not my nurse any longer, and I'll feel like an old man on the trip if you call me Mr. Cameron. We are, I think, only a few years apart in age."

Abby couldn't argue with anything he had said, and it was becoming an effort to call him Mr. Cameron when she always thought of him as Paul.

"Alright, I'll call you Paul. Are you going to call me Abby?" Her look was innocent as she asked the question, but he was not fooled.

"Sometimes," he answered her in all honesty and smiled. To him she was Red, and he didn't think anything could stop him from calling her that.

Abby smiled back, and the two of them spent the rest of the evening discussing Bayfield.

34

Ross paced the train station platform like a caged animal. Hoping he would want to go north with them, Paul hadn't expected such an enthusiastic response and was glad he hadn't asked any further in advance. Ross would never have withstood the wait.

"Is that the train?"

"Ross, that's the fourth time you've asked," Abby said with amusement.

"Oh, is it? I guess I'm a little excited."

Paul and Mr. Beckett were a little further down the platform, and Mr. Beckett's words were the same as his son's. "I don't know when I've seen him so excited. He's quite taken with you and Abby. I hope he'll behave himself."

"I'm sure we'll all get along fine. Ross has a heart for God and His will, and I know it'll be a good trip."

"Yes, well," Mr. Beckett stumbled a bit each time he was reminded that this man was a preacher, "you're sure you have enough money?"

"We're fine, thank you."

"I've given Ross some. Don't hesitate to ask him."

"Thank you, Mr. Beckett. You have done more than enough. Please let me tell you again how I appreciate the way you opened your home to us. I praise God for your and Mrs. Beckett's hospitality, and I'll be remembering you in prayer long after we're apart."

Sam Beckett looked at the younger man in silence and felt once again amazed. Paul Cameron went against every preconceived notion he had ever had about preachers. He was not helpless or feminine or trying to shove a Bible down your throat, but he was a man of God—there was no doubt about that. Ross could do a lot worse than Paul and Abby as traveling companions—a lot worse.

He would have trusted Abby with Ross' life, and now with Paul Cameron by her side, he hoped his son would come back ready to settle into a career of some kind.

Liking the idea of Ross becoming a lawyer, Sam nevertheless said little. Just about the time he confirmed the idea in his own mind, Ross was sure to change his. There was no predicting young people these days.

The train rumbled into the station not much later. Sam shook hands with Paul and hugged Abby. They climbed aboard and took seats. Ross and Sam faced one another outside the train.

"You look like I'm never coming back, Dad," Ross joked lightly.

"Oh, I think you'll be back. I just don't know who you'll be when you get here." Ross looked at him in confusion. "Don't get me wrong, Ross. The changes are good ones. They're just surprising."

"I sometimes can't believe it myself," Ross said, now understanding his dad's meaning. "I mean, I'm learning things about myself I never knew and well, like you said, changing."

"Well, son, you're young and it was bound to happen."

"What's happened to me, Dad, has nothing to do with my age," Ross told his father in the most serious voice Sam had ever heard from him. "Anyone can know Christ, Dad. And He is the One who makes the changes." Suddenly Ross' arms were tight around his father. He gave him a long, hard hug. Sam heard the words "I love you" whispered in his ear just before Ross broke away and boarded the train.

They waved to Sam from the windows as the train pulled out, heading north. Ross sat back in his seat facing Abby. Paul was at his side by the window.

"Ross, did you get a chance to talk with your mom?" Abby asked in kindness.

"Yes, Abby, thanks. I'll tell you about it later."

Abby accepted this without question and Ross appreciated it. Having just said good-bye to his father, he felt a little teary and was afraid that talking of his mother would have him crying on the train.

Ross had never seen his father so vulnerable. The relationship between them was a little different now, as it was bound to be. Ross felt a pang of hurt at even the slightest estrangement from his parents, whom he loved dearly. He couldn't be sorry for seeing his need for a Savior and believing in Jesus Christ. Remembering his conversation with his mother, he prayed right then that someday he would have the words to cause her to think about eternity.

"Mom, I'm leaving tomorrow, and I don't want to go with you upset."

"But I'm not upset with you, Ross," Lenore had genuinely assured him.

"Well, maybe not, but ever since I told you and Dad about my salvation, well, you've been preoccupied."

"I guess it does make me feel a little strange to have you talk about God the way you do and pray at meals and such."

"Does it feel funny when you talk to Abby or Paul?"

"No, I guess it doesn't. But Paul is a minister and Abby was a minister's wife. I guess I somehow expect it of them. With you I just feel as though there is something you and I can't share, and we've always been so close."

Ross had been unsure of what to say. In her unsaved state there was indeed something they could not share. But he still loved her unreservedly.

She went on while he was still thinking of an answer. "I feel like you don't need us anymore."

"Oh, Mom! Never think that. I need you and love you so much. I'll miss you more than I can say on this trip, and I hope we can talk more when I get back."

Ross could still envision his mother's indecisive face, but she had hugged him tightly and told him she loved him too. Now Ross' father, probably back home by now, was in Ross' mind as he had left him—standing by the train waving with a mixture of confused joy on his face. "It's no wonder he looked confused," Ross thought with regret, "I've probably never told him that I love him."

As the train rocked down the tracks, Ross prayed for his parents. "Please, Lord, lead them to You. Use me to show them their need. Please, God, save my parents."

35

The trip was not too long, but the nearer the three travelers came to Bayfield, the more restless Paul became. The men had dozed for a time, but now the inactivity of hours on the train was making Paul squirm. Abby strongly suspected he was a bit unsure of his reception, and it was showing in the way he constantly shifted and with his preoccupied stare out the window.

Abby searched her mind for some subject with which to distract him. They had exhausted just about every one, and the basket of food Anna had sent along was nearly depleted.

"Paul, you've never shared how you came to be a pastor," Abby said as the thought suddenly came to her. "Had you wanted to preach from boyhood?"

"I wish I had known from boyhood," Paul said with a small smile. Abby looked at him so expectantly, and he could see that Ross was all ears too, so Paul began his story.

"My mother died when I was nine, and even though I knew she was going to heaven, I was devastated. The only thing that helped me hang on was knowing I would see her again. I think it was then that I started wondering about people who didn't know whether they would see their loved ones again. But I was pretty young and not able to really handle such thoughts. I did my best not to dwell on them.

"Well, anyway, my older sister Julia took over most of the responsibilities of the house then. We were all a little busier, but she did most of the work even though she was only 12. She still had to go to school, but she was expected to cook and clean plus make trips to town for supplies. Well, I think she was around 15 when she came home from town one day with a sparkle in her eyes. She had seen our neighbor John MacDonald in the general store. Now, I don't think that Julia seeing Mac—that's what we call him—was anything new. But Mac hadn't really *seen* Julia for a few years, and suddenly she was this tall, beautiful young woman.

"That night after supper Mac came to the ranch. It was more than a little obvious he was interested in Julia. Julia returned his attention; in fact, she didn't take her eyes off him all evening.

"Unfortunately, Mac wasn't a believer. He was honest, hardworking and a good neighbor, but he didn't know Christ. My father was adamant about Julia not seeing him again.

"Julia was crushed, but I don't think she even considered disobeying. Oh, she was always full of mischief—still is, but she wasn't willful to our father. Well, the next night Mac came again. My father kept all of us boys off the porch. I don't know what she said, but Mac didn't stay very long, and when Julia came in she went right to her room for the night.

"I'll never forget the change in her after that. I guess because I lost my mother when I was so young, Julia just naturally filled her place in my life. At the time I never stopped to think that she had needs of her own. She just always took care of us, made sure I washed behind my ears, had clean clothes, and well, was just a mother to me. But all of that changed the day after Mac left.

"Julia was preoccupied, and I felt like I'd lost my mother all over again. She didn't talk to me very much or check up on me like she had. I knew it had something to do with Mac, but no one would tell me anything and I felt helpless and rejected.

"I wasn't the only one to see a difference in her. My father lit into her one night about her moping around the house and threatened to work her fingers to the bone if she didn't work on her attitude and get back in the family. Even as much as I wanted the 'old' Julia back, I thought he'd been pretty rough on her.

"Things did get better then—better for everyone but Julia. She bent over backward to keep things in order for all of us and totally neglected herself. She never sat down to a meal with us unless my father insisted, and she began losing weight. She would play games with me anytime I wanted, but I knew it was keeping her from her work and I stopped asking.

"I can't remember how much time went by, but I came in the kitchen one day to find her on the floor. I thought she was dead. By the time I found my dad in the barn, I was hysterical. She was still unconscious when my dad and brothers ran to the house. Luke and Silas went for our grandfather who was the doctor in town.

"I didn't want to leave Julia. I was sure she was going to die, and I knew if I left her side it would happen while I was gone." Paul fell silent for a moment as he thought of those days by Julia's bed. The helpless feeling he had experienced when Corrine was bedridden came rushing back to Paul so fast it brought a pain to his chest.

Abby and Ross studied him. Abby would have allowed Paul the silence. Being more informed than Ross, she knew where his thoughts were centered. But Ross was totally absorbed in the story.

"Was Julia alright?"

The question brought Paul back to the present, and he was thankful for the distraction. "Yes, Ross, she was alright, but it took about three days. My grandmother came and ran the household, and my grandfather only left her side to see to emergency situations. I kept a constant vigil near her; in fact, I cried uncontrollably if they tried to remove me.

"Well, Julia's fever broke and still I stayed by her side. As she regained her strength, she began to talk with me. I was amazed to learn she wasn't upset with our father. Her breakdown was over what Mac thought of her. As I look back now, I'm sorry for the pain Julia had to go through. But I'm not sorry for the result.

"A family discussion was held when Julia was finally out of bed, and my father apologized to Julia for his insensitivity. Silas' chores in the barn were cut down, and he began to help in the house. The whole thing brought us closer together when, as a family, we began to pray for John MacDonald. Months went by. Julia had some bleak days, but one miraculous Sunday morning Mac walked into church. I said hello to him after the service, but I don't think he let anyone else get near him.

"Things went on like that for a while. The only change was Julia making us late because she insisted we drive at a snail's pace so as not to mess her hair. And then our father surprised all of us by asking Mac to Sunday dinner. It was a disaster. Julia burned everything she put on the table—including herself, because she was watching Mac and not where she was pouring the burned gravy."

"Oh, Paul," Abby laughed. "I can't believe it was that bad."

"I swear to you, Abby. Everything that could go wrong did!"

"And this is all leading up to your becoming a pastor?" Ross looked as skeptical as his question sounded.

"Believe it or not, yes. After Mac left that day, Julia was inconsolable. She cried in her bedroom for hours. My father finally sent for Gram. She and Julia were in that room for a long time. I'll never forget the scene that day. All of us boys were sitting in the kitchen when Gram came out alone. She spoke directly to my father.

"'She's in love with Mac, Joseph, deeply in love. But it's more than that. She can't stand the thought that he'll die and go to hell. She said dinner was a fiasco and that even if you did invite him back next Sunday, he probably wouldn't come.'

"I couldn't get my grandmother's words out of my head. Mac was going to hell if he didn't realize his need for Christ.

I began to pray that day as I've never prayed before. I begged God to save Mac. And then something happened that I never would have dreamed.

"Mac came to church and dinner each Sunday after that, and on one of those days the two of us ended up alone together on the back porch. I was only about 12 at the time, but I knew I was supposed to talk with Mac about salvation. I was scared. Mac had always been so nice, but he was such a big man and I was a little afraid of how he would react if I told him he was a sinner and needed Christ. I really didn't need to be afraid of anything because Mac was ready and I was the tool God used that day. I quoted some verses to Mac and he, without hesitation, prayed and trusted in Jesus Christ. I worked hard at not letting him see my tears, but he was crying too and we ended up laughing."

"So you knew then you wanted to be a pastor?"

"No, Ross, not right then, but it was a turning point. When I was older and didn't know what I wanted to do with my life, that day on the porch kept coming to mind. Mark, from as far back as I could remember, wanted to be a doctor. Luke and Silas' strongest desire was to work with the horses. Julia married Mac and I went through some indecisive years, but God kept reminding me of that remarkable day. I never had more peace in my life than when I told my family I was going to seminary. I knew I wanted to spend my life telling people like Mac that they needed God."

As though Paul had planned it, the train rolled into Bayfield just as he was finishing his story. Within minutes the three of them stood on the station platform. Ross looked about with the avid interest of a teenager, whereas Paul and Abby were both quiet, alone with their thoughts. Wishing she could take Paul's hand and reassure him, Abby felt all would be well. Paul, as the memories began to assail him, wondered if he was going to be able to handle this task God had called him to do.

36

Abby felt Paul's hand move beneath her arm as he began to lead them away from the train. They each had small traveling bags. Ross, being the gentleman, took Abby's. Bayfield was nestled on an inlet of Lake Superior and carried with it an air of the lake trade.

As Paul steered his traveling companions in the direction of Lloyd Templeton's home, the bay with its water-going vessels came into view. Gulls flapped their wings and called to one another in a high-pitched cry overhead. Ross was enthralled.

"I've never been this far north before." His voice sounded a bit breathless. "This is beautiful, I mean, being right on the water and all."

A few large ships were in port, and the three of them stood and watched the activity on the docks. Barrels and crates were being unloaded. Lines being thrown with shouts and some laughter. The day was a scorcher, and Abby didn't envy the men their backbreaking task of unloading the ships.

Tightening the hand that was still holding Abby's arm, Paul indicated he was ready to walk on. Abby wondered if maybe she didn't hold a bit of security for him. She prayed as they walked—he was so quiet.

They began to climb a hill, and the silence among them deepened. The incline became rather steep before Paul stopped in front of a large two-story home. Abby, having been so intent on her walking, was not prepared for arriving at the house so quickly. And she was still worried about Paul's silence.

"Paul," Abby stopped him with a hand to his arm, "maybe you should go in alone. I mean, if Ross and I will be in the way ... what I'm trying to say is—"

"I want you both with me." Paul cut her off, thinking as he did that he could kiss her for her thoughtfulness. He was feeling very unsure of his welcome but no matter what was said to him, including being told outright that he wasn't welcome, he still wanted them along.

About an hour later, Paul sat opposite Lloyd Templeton in the study of their home—a home where he had been welcomed without hesitation.

"Some might say, Paul, that you've been dealt a bad hand. But I'm a God-fearing man and I don't believe God handles His children that way. But the fact is that everyone knew the truth about Corrine except you."

Upon arriving, Mrs. Templeton had shown Ross and Abby where they could freshen up, and Paul and Mr. Templeton had retired to the study. Paul relayed his experiences since they last saw each other and Mr. Templeton had listened with compassion, speaking only when Paul had finished.

"I hate the fact that I was not there that night. They should never have allowed you to leave, but Hugh and Rose were in no shape to reach out to you, not that that excuses the way everything was handled. Never accepting Corrine's illness, Hugh didn't allow anyone to talk about it. I just couldn't bring myself to tell you how serious it was."

The older man stopped talking and watched Paul deal with all he had said. His next words gave Paul hope for a reconciliation with the congregation.

"I'm not saying your leaving the church without notice was right, Paul, but we all understood. You came before us week after week, and we would have been blind not to see the way you were feeling about Corrine. We also saw Corrine more happy than we ever had and Hugh attending church on a regular basis. When you two were married, everyone went against what they knew to be true and prayed for a miracle, because a miracle was what it would have taken, Paul.

"Now I'm not saying that God doesn't have enough miracles to go around, Paul, but it just wasn't His will that Corrine live. I think you know that now."

Paul nodded silently, thanking God in his heart for this godly man's words.

"We were a little lost at first when you left, but we continued to meet each Sunday morning for prayer. The first person we prayed for each week was our absentee pastor. Everyone still believes you belong here."

Paul was beginning to feel a little short of breath as he realized what Lloyd was saying to him. He still had a church! They didn't think him gone, only absent for a while. "Thank You, Lord. Thank You, Lord."

Lloyd smiled at the look on his face. "Did you think God would desert us way up here in the north? He knew you were—and still are—the man for this church."

37

The sky was growing dusky the next evening when Paul stood outside the Griffin home and marked their name off his list.

He had gone to the home of each member of his congregation that day to talk with them and apologize. Not one family had turned him away. Even though his legs were throbbing, he was exuberant that he could step into the pulpit in the morning with a clear heart.

Paul was about to return the list to his pocket when a name at the bottom caught his attention: Aaron Johnson. Paul remembered then that he hadn't been home when he stopped. Aaron Johnson was a widower with two children and not a regular attender. Paul was determined to talk with him nonetheless. "Maybe in the morning," he thought as he started for home. "I can single him out before the service starts."

Paul was back at the Templetons in time for supper, and everyone listened with joy to his excited account of the day. He shared many of his conversations and ended by saying, "I've been selling the people of Bayfield short with my fears of rejection. Everyone has forgiven me without hesitation." Paul stopped because tears were clogging his throat. The women at the table were in the same condition, and they all ate in silence until dessert.

"The only person I missed," Paul said through bites of cobbler, "was Aaron Johnson."

"Oh, Paul, he was here today," May Templeton cut in. "He just stayed a few minutes to drop something off. But I told him you were back and introduced him to Ross and Abby."

"Well, I'm glad he knows I'm back. Maybe I can speak with him in the morning."

— ✣ —

"And Joseph said unto them, 'Fear not; for am I in the place of God?' " These were Paul's first words in his sermon the next morning. Aaron Johnson had come, and Paul spoke with him. There had been much visiting and sharing which Paul had no intention of interrupting even though they were late starting. As he was coming to expect of these fine people, they made Ross and Abby feel most welcome.

But now a few songs had been sung and some announcements made and Paul was ready to preach. "The words I just read to you out of Genesis 50 were the words Joseph spoke to his brothers. They are words of forgiveness— forgiveness to these brothers who, in a jealous rage, sold him to a caravan going to Egypt where he was made into a slave.

"He spent years away from his family, some of those years full of toil and heartache. But when a famine came over the land and he found his own brothers before him asking for food, he took no revenge. And even when their father died and the brothers were sure the time for revenge had come, Joseph spoke these words.

"I don't share this verse with you because I liken myself to Joseph. I left of my own accord, in sin against my God. But the forgiveness Joseph showed his brothers is the forgiveness you have shown to me this day." Paul's voice broke, and he took a moment to compose himself.

"There are a few things Joseph and I have in common, and one is that God never left his side as He never left mine. Daily He urged me to surrender my bitterness and hurt, and I fought Him. But lovingly, in a way only God can master, He tenderly broke through my wall of pain, and with the confession of my sins I have full fellowship again."

Abby felt a headache coming on in her effort to hold back tears as she watched this man stand open and vulnerable before his flock. Beside her, Ross swallowed convulsively in an effort to remove the clog in his own throat. All around them handkerchiefs were coming out and some people were openly crying. Abby wondered if Paul would be able to continue.

"I'll close by repeating what I said about leaving of my own accord and in sin. But again, as Joseph was, I am now in the place where God wants me, and I wouldn't be were it not for your prayers and forgiveness. For this, I thank you from the bottom of my heart."

The people stood then and, with Paul leading, most sang the doxology with tears streaming down their faces. Paul looked down as he sang, and Abby saw the way his eyes were filled with peace. She couldn't contain her tears any longer.

Sunday dinners were very late that day as everyone stayed for over an hour to visit and share. Abby was invited to join a quilting bee that was to be held the next week. Ross met two young men near his age and they made plans to fish.

When things began to clear, Paul sent people away with handshakes and hugs. He knew pain and disappointment that Corrine's parents were not there, and also knew that even though they weren't on his list, he had to go see them very soon.

Lloyd and May went on in their buggy, and Ross and Abby stayed with Paul as he locked the church. Descending the church steps, he went right to Ross, his hand extended.

"Thanks, Ross, for being here. It means more than I can say."

"The pleasure is all mine, Pastor Cameron," Ross answered with a sincere smile.

Paul then turned to Abby, and she smiled and extended her hand. Reaching for that hand, he didn't shake it but pulled her into his arms. It took a moment for a surprised Abby to react, but then she hugged him back with her heart overflowing.

When they parted, Paul's voice was strained. "Thanks, Red." Abby could only nod before she turned away, knowing if she looked at him she would start to cry again.

The excitement of the day seemed to drain everyone's strength, and all five people at Lloyd Templeton's home spent the remainder of the day in quiet rest.

38

Paul's entire body shook with emotion two days later as he stood before the home of his wife's parents. Memories assailed him like a full-force gale, robbing him of breath for a moment: the first time he had walked up these steps to find Corrine sick and hurting... his wedding day at her bedside... believing with all his heart she would get out of that bed. And then the night she died and he walked away from this house telling himself he would *never* return.

But here he was, and the pain was nearly overpowering. Knowing the raw feeling inside would not abate until he confronted his in-laws, he started up the steps.

"I'd like to see Mr. and Mrs. Templeton, please," Paul stated when a woman opened the door. She wordlessly stepped aside for his entrance, and Paul waited in the very room he had found his thin, sick Corrine and had proposed to her.

"Hello, Paul."

At the very softly spoken words, Paul spun from his place by the fireplace to find Mrs. Templeton. She looked in good health, but there were lines around her eyes and mouth he had never noticed before. Paul opened his mouth to speak.

"If you've come here to apologize for anything, Paul, please don't."

"You can understand why I want to, can't you?"

"Yes, I suppose I can, but never once were you treated fairly in our pursuit to see Corrine happy, and for that Hugh and I owe you more apology than we could ever offer. Hugh is not here right now, but then, I don't suppose he would be able to say the words anyhow."

The two of them sat in silence before Mrs. Templeton

continued. "I hope for your sake, Paul, that you never have an unwell child. Corrine was sickly from birth. You become a little more attached to them every time they have a brush with death and survive. And then the time comes when they don't make it, and you realize you knew all along it would happen but you had deluded yourself into believing otherwise. I'm afraid that's where you came in.

"Corrine fell for you the minute she laid eyes on you, and when I saw the happiness you brought her I selfishly ignored your needs in my effort to see her happy, no matter how briefly. I don't blame you if you hate us. I hate myself. I haven't been able to talk to God since you left."

Paul's eyes closed in agony, and he moved close to her on the settee. He held her hand and spoke. "There is no hate in my heart—that I promise you. And the fact that I am the reason you haven't had fellowship with the Lord hurts like a knife in my side."

"Oh, it's not your fault. I never meant that—"

"It *is* my fault, but I won't argue with you. I should have stayed, but that's over. I've been away and now I'm back. And I'll do anything I can to see you restored to fellowship with God, a heavenly Father we both know can salve every hurt with His unconditional healing love."

"It's been so awful." The older woman began to cry brokenly.

"I know, but His arms are always opened wide." Paul said this, and then watched as Rose Templeton bowed her head in prayer. He prayed silently to himself for God's comfort and healing for all of them as they continued to face life after Corrine's death.

"Please, God, please," Paul heard her whisper, and instantly saw himself on his back in bed at the Becketts' house, uttering those same words and wanting desperately to be restored. Opening his eyes, he looked at his mother-in-law in concern when she began to cry very hard.

He held her hand and patted it gently, but her crying was

becoming hysterical. When she groped for her handkerchief, Paul quickly handed her his own, but the crying
didn't cease. He heard someone in the hallway and debated
about going for help. If anything, her sobbing was more
severe, and Paul prayed for wisdom to comfort her.

He was just about to go for help when Hugh Templeton
walked through the door. He hardly spared a glance in
Paul's direction as he came to his wife. Paul wouldn't have
believed the man's voice could be so gentle if he hadn't
heard it with his own ears.

"Rosie, Rosie—it's alright. I'm here now. Try to stop
crying. You'll make yourself sick." Hugh's arms were around
his wife, and he continued to talk softly in her ear as he
pulled her to her feet.

Paul stood helplessly as he watched the concerned husband lift his wife into his arms and carry her from the room.
Once alone he ran a distracted hand through his hair and
spoke to the empty room. "What have I done?"

Paul debated about leaving, but concern for Corrine's
mother caused him to pace around indecisively. He had
decided to come back another time when Hugh Templeton's frame filled the doorway. Paul steeled himself for the
anger he was sure would be directed at him.

"I don't know what you've done," Paul held his breath as
the older man spoke, "but I want to thank you."

Would this man never cease to surprise him?

"I can see I've shocked you, but the truth is Rose hasn't
cried since the night Corrine died, and I've worried about
her. I think she'll be getting better now. I've put her to bed
and well, you can come back another time or maybe see
her at church.

Paul could only stare.

Hugh Templeton nodded to the silent young man and left
the room. Paul made his way to the front door in something
of a state of shock and was almost outside when Hugh
Templeton spoke from behind him.

"Our family graveyard is out to the west, beyond the flowers. Corrine is buried there." Without waiting for thanks, the man disappeared into the back of the house and Paul continued outside.

39

Corrine Maria Cameron
1869-1890
Beloved Wife and Daughter

Paul looked in silence at the words carved into the stone. It was awful to think of her body beneath the ground. But then *she* wasn't really there; she was in heaven where there was no more pain.

He lowered his body slowly to the grassy knoll and didn't try to pray; in fact, he tried not to think at all. The sun was in a mid-morning position, and the day promised to be warm. There were a few other graves nearby, but Paul took no notice of them. Someone keeps things cared for up here, he noted absently as he looked at the well-trimmed area which boasted a few flowers.

"She would have been 21 by now, Lord," Paul spoke softly in the breeze that had begun to stir. "I knew her such a short time, and yet she taught me so much. She would have been disappointed to know I ran away. She always handled her pain with a smile."

Tears ran from Paul's eyes and he felt such despair at not being able to see her again and tell her he loved her. Oh, he wouldn't have wanted her to come back to her pain, but he had fallen so deeply in love with her and had had her such a short time.

And now there was Abby. "Corrine," he spoke through his tears. "I would have been faithful to you all the days of my life, but you're gone now and I really think Abby and I need each other. It feels almost adulterous to sit at your grave and speak of another woman but—"

Paul didn't finish the words before he began to sob openly. He had cried many tears for the loss of his wife and

148

each time found them healing. But being at her grave, wondering who performed the ceremony that he should have attended, and thinking of the sweet love they had shared for so short a time made his heart feel like it was breaking.

And in the midst of it all was Abby's face. Did that mean he didn't love Corrine anymore? His confusion was great and his tears intensified. Before he realized it, his body gave way to emotional exhaustion.

Hours later Lloyd stood a few feet away and looked at the prone body of his pastor, a young man he loved and respected. He knew he would be in the same position if that had been May lying there and with him seeing her grave for the first time.

With a gentle hand he shook Paul's shoulder. "Come on, son, let's go home. May's got some lunch for you, and then I think you could use a rest."

Paul looked for a moment in confusion at the older man before rising and going with him down the hill. Back at the house he talked with no one and ate some lunch before retiring to his bed. He wondered, as he drifted off to sleep, if Abby had ever seen Ian's grave.

40

Abby had known it would come, but that didn't make it any easier. There was no way Paul could come back to this town and not be affected by his memories. She wondered how she would feel if she went back to Canada—probably just as distracted and seemingly remote when she faced the past as Paul was right now. But she missed the other Paul—the one who laughed easily and didn't seem elsewhere even while in a crowded room.

She had accompanied Paul up here as planned, and knew that he would look after Ross, who was in reality old enough to look after himself. The time had come for her to go home.

She would write to the Becketts and ask them to send the rest of her things to Michigan, and then she would head home after she stopped in Bruce Mines. She would know then how Paul was feeling right now. All the memories of her life with Ian would meet her, good and bad.

She would wait until after Sunday. The quilting bee was Saturday morning, and she wanted to attend. Leaving Paul would be hard enough as it was, and somehow she thought staying to hear him preach one more time would ease the pain. He had such a special way with words, so clearly showing his love of God—and that voice!

Abby concentrated for a moment on what his laugh sounded like—very deep and quiet. Instantly she could feel his arms around her, strong and warm as when he had hugged her outside the church. She knew the hug from his perspective had been one of gratitude, but she was feeling more than gratitude, and she couldn't seem to help herself.

"Oh, Ian, I'm so confused. What we had was so special." But her room didn't answer.

Her next thought was of Aaron Johnson. He had come by that morning and stayed for quite some time. Paul had been out, but Aaron had visited with Ross and May. Abby had found his two children, Gwen and James, adorable. Abby had been leery after finding out he was a widower, but his manner was so shy and unpretentious. When his children displayed the same shy manner she lost some of her reserve.

But she couldn't marry a man because she felt sorry for him and his children. It would be wonderful if he could find a wife, but Abby knew she was not that woman.

"Yes, Lord, I think you want me to go home. I guess I halfway hoped that Paul and I would someday be together, but he needs to be concentrating on his life here and the church. He doesn't need me hanging around."

Abby knew she was feeling sorry for herself. Part of the problem was that she should have been asleep half an hour ago. She resettled herself on the pillow and decided to pray herself into slumber.

Down the hall, Ross and Paul were readying for bed. Paul sat on the edge of his bed to pull off his shoes. He glanced up to find Ross lying in his own bed staring intently at him.

"When Abby first came to Hayward," Ross began without warning, "I fell for her—hard. I still think she's wonderful, but I know she's not the woman God has for me."

Ross paused, and Paul sat in silence waiting for the point he was sure was coming.

"It was hard for me at first—I mean when I knew she hadn't fallen for me. But then she told me of Christ, and I know that's why she came. And well, I still think she's really special, and I guess I would like to see her loved and cared for. Every time I pray for her, you come to mind."

Paul looked at him without comment or change of expression, and Ross went on.

"Now I know it can't be easy for you being up here where you met your wife, and I don't expect you to confide in me because none of this is really any of my business. I know that Abby was really in love with her husband, but somehow I just think you two would be really good for each other. I'm sorry if you think I'm putting my nose in where it doesn't belong." Ross seemed to run out of words, and he looked a little uncomfortable as he finished.

"I don't think you are being nosey, and I appreciate that you care for Abby, but I would like to know what brought all of this on."

Ross hesitated for a long moment. "There was a man here today—Aaron Johnson. He visited with Abby for over two hours."

"How does Abby know Aaron Johnson?" Paul asked in genuine confusion.

"Remember, he came by that first day, and then he talked to her again at church on Sunday. And well, today when he was here, they sort of hit it off. That is, he didn't take his eyes off her the whole time he was here, and she was delighted with his children."

Ross watched Paul's face carefully. He was so good at hiding his feelings, but then Ross saw it—just the tiniest flicker of concern in his eyes. Ross lay back in satisfaction then. He wasn't good with words like Paul, and that flicker told Ross that Paul had understood what he meant.

The men didn't talk further, but Paul's mind was certainly full as he turned down the lamp. It was long after Ross' breathing had evened into sleep that Paul finished praying and was able to find his own rest.

41

"Paul, can I talk to you a moment?"

"Certainly," Paul answered as he followed Lloyd into the study. It was after breakfast the next morning, and Paul was headed to spend some time with Abby. He had done much thinking in the night and come to some peaceful conclusions, but he really needed to talk with her and see how she was feeling.

He didn't want to be rude to Lloyd, but had hoped to see Abby before she left for the quilting bee at Loni Griffin's.

"How are you doing, Paul?" Lloyd spoke after they both were seated.

"Very well, thank you," wondering, as he answered, why he had really been called into the study.

"It's sure a pleasure to have Ross and Abby here."

"Yes, they're both very special to me."

"Is Abby by any chance extra-special?" The older man rushed on before Paul could even take a breath. "Oh now, I know you're still hurting over Corrine and I don't want to be insensitive, Paul, but Abby told May this morning that it's time she went home. To tell the truth, I guess we both got the feeling she was going to be a little more permanent."

If there had been a single doubt in Paul's mind over what to do with his feelings for Abby, they were banished in that instant. He couldn't let her leave. Maybe they needed a little more time together to get to know one another, but there was no way he could allow her to leave.

"Thanks, Lloyd, for telling me. I've got to run now. I want to catch Abby before she goes to the Griffins." Paul rushed out the door leaving it standing wide, and in a few minutes May came in.

"Did you have a chance to ask him?"

"Yes, and I don't even want to tell you how quickly he rushed out of here and have you say 'I told you so.'"

"Oh no, dear, I would never say that. I'll settle for you telling me I'm always right." Her look was one of such feigned innocence that Lloyd laughed. May joined him even as they both wanted to know what was going on with their young pastor right then.

— —

Paul rushed along the street that he had just seen Abby and Priscilla Dayton head down. They were talking companionably as they went and were surprised when Paul seemed to appear out of nowhere.

"Good morning, ladies. May I walk you to the Griffins?"

"Oh certainly, Pastor Cameron," Priscilla said with genuine delight. "We would feel honored. Wouldn't we, Abby?"

"Oh yes," Abby answered absently, wondering what Paul was up to. She could see he was trying very hard to act casual, but Abby wasn't fooled. His smile was a bit strained, and she knew he would have walked much faster had he been alone. In fact, she thought, why wasn't he alone? Surely he must have better things to do with his time than walk two women to a quilting bee. A repressed air nearly reverberated about him as though he had exciting news he was bursting to tell.

Abby's confusion grew as they walked and Priscilla made conversation. Abby noticed that Paul's answers were brief, and he kept shooting glances her way.

It didn't take very long to reach their destination. Priscilla went right to the door, but Abby hung back with a quick explanation. "I'll be right there, Priscilla. Don't wait for me."

The other woman gave her a quick wave and headed up the steps and through the door. Paul and Abby walked to the corner of the house for a little privacy from the front windows, and Abby spoke.

"Is something wrong, Paul?"

Definitely, Paul thought, glad that she had not gone right inside, but wondered how he was going to tell her what was on his mind. A few moments of silence elapsed, leaving Abby more confused than ever. Paul was about to ask Abby how she liked Bayfield when he caught sight of Aaron Johnson coming out of the barrel-making shop. He turned suddenly and in a quiet voice, laced with panic, blurted out: "Abby, will you marry me?"

"What?" Abby fairly shrieked at him.

"I said, will you marry me?"

"Paul," Abby said, her voice dropping low, her hurt very evident, "I don't find that the least bit funny."

"It's no joke, Abby. I want you for my wife. And what's more, I think God wants it too."

Abby could only gawk at him. Where had such a proposal come from? Had he taken leave of his senses? She tried to think reasonably as to why he would do this, but her thoughts were a whirl of confusion.

All she could think to ask was "Why?"

"Because I think we would do very well together." His voice was very logical, and Abby was cut to the quick that he said nothing whatsoever about love.

"But Paul," she said with quiet pain, bringing up the subject that had never quite left her mind, "you don't even find me attractive. You don't like my size or the smell of my bath oil for that matter."

Paul, he reprimanded himself, you did such damage with those cruel, thoughtless words.

"Oh, Red," Paul's voice dropped to a murmur and his eyes filled with tenderness as he looked at her, "I find you lovely beyond description. Those words were spoken by a bitter, self-absorbed man who was fighting the attraction he was feeling for his nurse. And even at that, I never meant for you to hear. All I can do is tell you that's not the way I feel and ask your forgiveness."

He watched her eyes soften at his words even as she bit her lip, trying to determine if he was being honest with her. Paul watched the way the sun bounced off her gorgeous red hair, and her huge gray eyes drew him like a magnet. He placed a hand beneath her chin and bent his head.

"Paul!" Abby said breathlessly as she stepped away from a touch she enjoyed. "We're on a public street."

Paul looked around in frustration, glad that she had more presence of mind than he did at the moment. He couldn't believe he had almost kissed her right here before the home of one of his parishioners.

"I need to get inside." Abby's voice cut quietly into the awkward moment and Paul's racing thoughts.

She didn't look at him as she spoke, and he could see her cheeks were aflame with embarrassment.

"I'll let you go, but please remember that nothing I said was meant as a joke and we still need to talk." When Abby didn't answer, Paul pursued the subject. "We will talk, won't we? I mean, I'm always a little afraid you're going to disappear out of my life as suddenly as you appeared."

"We can talk if you want." Abby's voice was subdued, and Paul knew how badly he had handled the whole thing.

"You won't leave when I'm not looking?"

"No," was Abby's answer, avoiding his eyes.

Paul hoped that she would look at him, and he stood watching as she mounted the stairs and knocked at the door. When the door was opened, she vanished inside without a backward glance. What a mess he had made of things. He moved slowly away from the house, one hand rubbing the back of his neck in frustration.

"Please, Lord," he prayed as he turned away from the house, "help me to make things right with the woman I love."

42

It was after lunch before Abby walked back to the Templetons. She had been asked to stay for noon dinner and, desperately needing the distraction, accepted.

Distraction—that was certainly a good way to describe the morning. She hadn't come across a group of such fun-loving ladies since she left her home church in Michigan. There had only been a few women she knew, and those she had met Sunday at church. The rest were ladies from all over town: some with little ones in tow, others pregnant, and more than one old enough to be her mother or possibly her grandmother.

Scissors were tucked away and laughter was plentiful as jokes and family stories were shared over lunch. Abby sat with Priscilla and found her to be a woman of discretion. Telling no one of Paul's accompanying them, she had asked privately if Abby had stayed outside because something was wrong. She accepted Abby's brief answer without question, and the subject was dropped.

It would be so easy to fit into this warm community, Abby's heart thought wistfully. And the Griffins' house was spacious and homey. Abby had never had a home of her own, and she let her mind wonder for a moment to what it would be like furnishing and keeping her own home.

But a warm community and possibly having a home of her own were not reasons to marry a man. Some would think her a sentimental fool in these times when many married out of necessity and not for love. But Abby knew she couldn't—wouldn't—marry for such shallow reasons. Then again, maybe her reason for marrying Paul wouldn't be so shallow. He would be very easy to love and, even if he didn't love her in return, Abby knew his belief in God would make him an honorable, faithful husband.

"Oh, Lord," Abby thought as she climbed the stairs to the house, "what would You have me do?"

Matty, the Templetons' cook, had the evening off. In her place, May and Abby outdid themselves with supper. May said she was feeling festive, so Abby set the dining table with the best dishes and flatware. May served pork roast and gravy with all the trimmings. There were strawberries over light biscuits with fresh cream for dessert, and Ross had thirds.

The dishes were cleared and everyone headed onto the back porch where a nice breeze was cooling the land and keeping the mosquitos at bay. Abby couldn't have relaxed for more than a few minutes when Ross jumped to his feet and said he had something to do. His footsteps could still be heard in the house when May asked Lloyd to look at some wallpaper samples with her.

Abby found herself alone with Paul, who had suddenly taken a great interest in his fingernails. Abby said nothing, and Paul didn't look in her direction for over five minutes from his place on the porch where he was leaning with one shoulder against a post.

"It's time for me to go home, Paul."

"And the question I asked you this morning?"

"I guess I didn't really take you seriously. Maybe you were serious at the time, but now that you've had all day—"

She had his full attention. The post was in the middle of his back now as he changed positions to see her. She could feel his eyes on her face as she looked out into the back-yard. Fear kept her from turning her head to look at him— fear of what emotion she would see there, fear of gaining his pity. She could take anything but that.

"I made quite a mess of things this morning, Red, and I'm sorry." Abby still refused to look at him.

"You wouldn't believe how angry I was at you when we first met because you were brimming with good health and

Corrine was dead." These words brought Abby's head around. "And then I found out I wasn't the only one to lose a mate. You had lost yours and still you trusted God. I was again angry because you were stronger than me."

"I wasn't strong at all," Abby said quietly.

"Yes, you were. You kept your hand in God's, and He enabled you to make it from day to day even in your pain. At first that was a threat to me, and then it began to be one of the things I most admired about you. That and the way you handled me—without fear or apology. If you had been weak in any way, I would have run right over the top of you.

"A few days after I arrived up here, I visited my wife's grave. I was nearly overcome with my pain and loss, but always in the back of my mind was your face. I felt adulterous, mourning over my dead wife and at the same time thinking of another woman. I've done little but pray about it since. I had come to some peaceful conclusions that I was going to take my time and share with you. But then May said you were leaving, and I rushed in and made a mess of things."

"Why didn't you tell me any of this earlier?"

Paul looked straight into her eyes as he answered. "Because I saw Aaron Johnson coming out of the factory and got scared."

"Aaron Johnson?"

Paul shrugged slightly. "I thought maybe you were returning his interest a little, and the thought made me more than a little anxious."

"I'm not interested in Mr. Johnson," Abby stated as she again turned her gaze to the yard.

"And me, Abby—could you be interested in me?"

The hesitancy she heard in his voice was heartbreaking; she couldn't turn to look at him as she began to talk.

"Ian Finlayson was a very special person, and I feel almost humbled that I was able to know him so well. He tried every day to live his life the way God would have. I not only loved him but admired and greatly respected him.

"To be angry at God for Ian's death would be to say to God that there had been no purpose in it, and that I could never do. A few months before Ian's death, we had a long talk and we made a promise to each other and to God. It may not seem in any way special to you, but we promised with all our hearts to always be used of God. For in being used of God you have opportunity to tell lost ones of His saving love.

"I didn't want to be in Baxter. The only reason I was there was because Ian was dead. And then your grandmother asked me to go to Hayward. I wanted to run away and pretend I hadn't heard her words. But I knew I had a promise to keep, and God wanted me in Hayward. And Ross was saved."

Abby's voice broke as she continued. "I know, Paul, that Ian smiled on that day because he would have gladly given his life to see someone come to Christ and, in a way, he did. Knowing all that I do about Ian and how wonderful he was, I wonder how I could be so drawn to you. It feels disloyal and confusing."

With the end of Abby's speech came her tears. Paul eased down onto the bench with her and pulled her against his chest. She did not resist him but turned her head into his shirt and cried.

Paul held her tenderly until her tears were spent. She used his handkerchief when she was ready to collect herself and pulled away from his embrace. Paul didn't move from his place but leaned down and gently kissed her cheek. There wasn't so much of a height difference when they were sitting, and Abby looked up to find his face close to hers.

"Listen to me, Red," he spoke softly into her upturned face. "There will always be a portion of your heart that belongs to Ian, just as a part of mine will to Corrine. But Ian and Corrine are not here and we are. Please believe me when I tell you I have thought and prayed much about this, and I think we belong together. I don't doubt for a minute we could love each other very much."

Abby's breath caught on his words.

"Tell me what that look on your face means."

"It's just so new. I mean, I knew how I was feeling about you, but until this morning I believed you thought I was a bossy red cow and—"

Abby stopped talking when Paul suddenly jumped to his feet and pulled her out to stand in the middle of the porch. Abby's face revealed bewilderment and then embarrassment as Paul looked down at her and then with measured tread slowly circled her. Abby didn't turn as he walked, but knew he was looking at her. She wanted to sink beneath the floor when he stopped in front of her only to circle around the other way.

When at last Paul stopped before Abby, her face was dull-red and her hands were clenching her skirt so tightly her knuckles were white. He bent nearly double to put his face on a level with hers.

"Ah, Red," his voice was soft, "I like the way you're put together"

Abby's whole body relaxed as she heard the sincere words, looked into those beautiful turquoise eyes, and felt her heart melt. She surprised both of them in the next instant by throwing her arms around Paul's neck and kissing him right on the mouth.

Paul's arms were beginning to surround her when Abby let go of him and scooted away. Her eyes were like saucers and her voice told of her shock when she said, "I didn't mean to do that."

"I think you did," Paul said with satisfaction as he started toward her.

"I have to go now."

"Abby!"

His answer was the slamming of the door. He let her go. She needed time and so did he.

43

The next few days were idyllic for Paul and Abby. On Sunday Paul was thrilled to see his in-laws come to church. Rose was smiling and Hugh was as unapproachable as ever, but they were there.

On Monday, Paul took Abby boating. She was hesitant at first, but once on the water had a wonderful time.

"You better pull your bonnet down a bit, Abby." The short redhead did as she was told.

"I hate freckles."

"Why, for goodness' sake?"

"Well, for the exact reason you just mentioned. I get millions of them when I'm in the sun. You must hate them too."

"No, I don't. I told you to pull your bonnet down because I'm afraid your fair skin will burn in this hot sun."

"Oh."

There was little noise as Paul maneuvered the boat into a shady inlet. The small borrowed craft rocked gently, and the sound of water slapping against the sides floated up to the occupants.

"You don't think very much of yourself do you, Red?"

"Why do you ask that?" Abby tried for a nonchalant tone, even as her heart raced in alarm. He had read something in her that she tried so hard to hide.

"Because you interpret most of the things I say about you negatively. At first I blamed it on my treatment of you in Hayward, but I think it started before that."

When Abby was silent, he went on. "Does my height bother you?"

"No!" Abby's surprise was very real. Such a thing had never occurred to her.

"Does the difference in our heights bother you?"

"No," she admitted slowly, "but I can't believe it doesn't bother you. I know that Corrine was tall and slim, and I just can't believe you find me attractive. And I also know that in your mind we covered all this, but I've always been a person who needed extra reassuring. I'm sure you won't be able to stand it when you really get to know me."

Abby could hardly believe she had admitted all that to him. But if they were taking some time to get to know each other and possibly be married, she wanted to be totally up front with him. It didn't change the fact that what she had just admitted was humiliating.

"You think I'm going to change my mind, don't you?"

Again he read her mind; it was very disconcerting.

"Abby, look at me. No, not my chin—my eyes." Gray eyes met blue-green ones. "Please marry me. Please be my wife and let me show you I'm not going to change my mind, and I don't find you repulsive as you obviously think I must."

"I'm afraid."

"I know you are. And I can't promise that I'll never die because only God knows that. But for as long as I have breath in my body, I'll be beside you."

"What if I'm not a good pastor's wife?"

"You've already been one."

"But Ian's flock was small—just a handful. What if the people here—"

"The people here love you and so do I."

There was not another person on the earth at that moment. Nothing else existed or mattered. Abby looked at the man across from her whose expression was tenderness itself and felt like she was drowning.

Paul was glad he said the words, but could see she still needed time. "It's okay. I'm not going to rush you, but I want you to know how I feel. Also know this: I would marry you today, and I'll be here when you need me."

Paul rowed them back to shore, and Abby spent the rest of the day and the evening in her room.

Paul missed her and wanted very much to go to her, but he comforted himself with the knowledge that she would be there in the morning and they could talk then.

But it was not to be. In the morning Abigail Finlayson was not to be found.

44

"Gone! What do you mean gone?"

"Her room is empty. I don't know where she is."

Paul looked thunderstruck by May's words as she stood by the dining room table. He looked to the faces of Lloyd and Ross and saw that their shock was as great as his own.

"When did she leave?"

"I don't know."

"Has her bed been slept in?"

"I don't know, Lloyd," May wrung her hands in frustration as she answered. "She always leaves her room as neat as a pin, and I just don't know."

Paul looked down at his plate without seeing it. His mind wouldn't function. She was gone. He had pushed her, and she had fled. The thought of her traveling alone sent pain pulsing through him even as he thought it was so unlike her to do this. He knew she was self-sufficient; he had seen that firsthand. Yet Paul couldn't bear the thought of her going unprotected.

"Excuse me." Paul's words were mumbled as he escaped the sorrow he saw in everyone's eyes.

"It just isn't like her," he heard Ross say as he exited the room.

"No, it isn't like her," Paul repeated again to himself as he found his feet taking him toward her room as though they had a mind of their own. He stepped within and found no comfort. It smelled like her—her jasmine bath oil.

Paul walked toward the dresser to where the small vial sat and the aroma grew stronger. His brows knitted together even as the scent floated to him. His eyes quickly scanned the room. On the table beside the bed sat Abby's Bible. With a quick reach of his arm, Paul threw open the wardrobe doors. He stared in growing horror at Abby's few dresses.

The bath oil, her clothes, her brush and comb were all here. Paul's breath quickened in fear. Someone had taken her. As though God had leaned down and whispered in his ear, he knew that someone was Ian Finlayson Sr. Until that moment the man had not really been a threat in Paul's mind, not having understood how much hate the man harbored for Abby.

Paul charged down the stairs to the dining room where the rest of the house was still gathered.

"All of her things are still in the room."

"Maybe she went for a walk," May offered, her voice small.

"Abby wouldn't go off without telling us," Ross said with conviction.

"Exactly!"

"So you think she's been abducted?"

"There are no signs of a struggle in her room, but yes, I do." Paul's face was grim.

May looked as though she was going to faint, and Ross' features reddened with anger.

"But who would take her—and how?" Lloyd asked, not wanting to believe what he was hearing.

"Her father-in-law, and I don't know how. It's a long story, but Abby told me he hated her after his son died. When we were still in Hayward, my grandmother wrote that an older man had been in Baxter asking for Abby."

"Where would he have taken her?"

"I don't know, but I'm headed out now to see if I can pick up their trail."

"We'll go with you. Come on, Ross."

The three men ran from the house leaving May in tears at the table. Over an hour later they were back at the house. Ross had gone to the train station, but no one had seen a woman of Abby's description. When he asked at the livery in town, the man said no one but the regulars had been in.

Paul and Lloyd had headed to the docks, and Paul was convinced that Abby and her father-in-law had left on a ship reported to be heading for Canada. It had gone out the night before, just after sunset.

Things had been quiet during the evening, and several men reported seeing a man with what appeared to be a small woman in an oversized cloak. He had purchased passage for two and kept a very close hold on his companion.

"Lloyd, will you please gather as much of the congregation as you can? I'll meet you all at the church in an hour."

The Templetons with Ross' help set off to see who they could find, and Paul went upstairs to his room. Once inside, he knelt slowly by the edge of the bed.

For nearly an hour Paul prayed. And when he rose, there wasn't a doubt in his mind about what he was to tell the people of his church.

He could tell when he arrived that Lloyd had informed everyone of the situation. "Thank you for coming. I think Lloyd has told you what's happened. Once I left here without a word to anyone, and I never plan to do that again. I'm leaving today, and I won't be back until I can find Abby.

"There is one other thing I want you to know. Before Abby was taken, I asked her to be my wife." The grim faces in the pews broke into smiles, and Paul felt as though a burden had been lifted from his shoulders. "Please cover us with your prayers."

Lloyd then led in a word of prayer for God's safekeeping on their pastor and Abby. Paul bought passage and left Bayfield that afternoon, confident of his course of action. It was no mistake that Abby entered his life when he needed her most, and now she needed him. With God's help, he wouldn't let her down.

45

"Be anxious for nothing, but in everything, by prayer and supplication with thanksgiving, let your requests be made known unto God." The words came to Paul's mind, and he wondered if there would ever be an instance when these words would be harder to obey.

"Abby, where will I find you?"

Paul whispered into the wind that blew over the deck of the ship that winged its way toward Canada. In his mind there was a plan, but even as he figured to disembark, get a train, and ride straight for Bruce Mines, he knew that Ian Sr. would not be sitting in his home simply waiting for someone to come.

Maybe he's taken her to their home and Mrs. Finlayson is taking care of her. The thought comforted Paul for a few moments, and then he thought of all the things a person can do when grieving or enraged. A shiver ran over him and he repeated Philippians 4:6 again.

Paul felt tears clog his throat when his mind conjured up the image of Abby sitting across from him in the boat. He doubted she was at all aware of the way her eyes pleaded with him to love and accept her just as she was. Well, he did love her, and even if it were in his power he wouldn't change a thing about her.

"Just keep her safe, Lord, and let me find her. I need her, and I promise to cherish her as we build a life in You."

Paul's words were once again snatched away by the wind, followed quickly by the single tear that streamed down his cheek.

— ✢ —

Abby flexed her shoulders and bit her lip against the pain. She ached from head to foot.

Without moving from her place against the wall, she could see the sun was setting. He hadn't brought her anything to eat that day, and she wondered if that was his plan now—to starve her to death. He certainly hated her enough.

She speculated as to what day it might be. It had taken a day to get back on land, or maybe it was two. She had lost all sense of time in that tiny room on the ship with no window and very little air. Although the trip to the farm hadn't taken that long, Abby panicked when he brought her out to this remote shed and not to the house.

Abby's hand went to the lump on her forehead where she had hit the ground and been knocked unconscious. She shouldn't have fought him, but when she saw that old shed nearly hidden by a windbreak of trees and way out in the field, she knew she had to get away because no one was going to find her.

If only she could have convinced him that what he was doing was wrong. It wasn't until they arrived in Canada that she realized he was sorry for what he was doing. Oh, his talk on the ship was angry and hateful, but once he had gotten her alone he seemed unable to carry out any of his threats. At one point he almost listened to her.

"You say you love your son, but can you honestly think that he would be pleased with the way you're treating his widow?" Abby's voice was pleading, and she saw his face soften some. "I loved Ian, but my death won't bring him back. If I thought that, I would gladly give you my life."

Abby really believed he was going to relent, but in the next instant he had a hold of her wrist and was once again dragging her along. He carefully avoided towns and farms where Abby could have asked for help. Now that she had sat here bruised and hurting for an undeterminable time, she wished she had fought against him at the Templetons. In a daze she tried to concentrate on how it had happened.

It was such an innocent desire—to want a breath of fresh air before bed, but there had been no fresh air as a meaty hand was clamped over her mouth. Before she knew it, she was in the backyard putting on a cloak at knife-point and following his commands without question.

Despair was quickly setting in as Abby prayed and sang herself into a fitful sleep.

The next morning she looked through blurry eyes to the small patch of sun streaming through the barred door that looked like part of an old prison cell. It had rained in the night, pouring down from the leaky roof, and not a single inch of the six-foot-square room had remained dry.

Abby's dress hung in wet folds as she crawled toward the door and into the sunlight. The breeze was stronger in front of the door, and she wondered if she had the strength to move back out of the way. Curling into a ball, Abby leaned against the bars of the door. She shivered almost violently even as sleep came back to claim her.

Ian Finlayson Sr. took another drink from the bottle in his hand. It was beginning to work—the pain was beginning to dull. A little bit longer and he wouldn't be able to visualize his son's face at all or picture his daughter-in-law as he'd left her.

His daughter-in-law—it was all her fault. But even as the thought occurred to him, he knew it wasn't true. She had loved Ian too, and nothing—certainly not her death—was going to bring him back.

Shame washed over him that he had actually wished her dead, and suddenly all interest in the drink was gone. He laid his head back against the wall and cried out for what must have been the millionth time, "Why did Ian have to die?" As usual, no answer came from the air, and the emptiness returned.

He was so sure if he could just get his hands on Abby that his fury would be appeased, but it hadn't worked that way at all. She had been hurting just like he was, and was very vulnerable in the face of his anger.

He put the bottle down and staggered to his feet. The morning sun outside the barn nearly blinded him, but he squinted at the house and moved toward it.

Mrs. Finlayson heard the back door open and turned from the stove in surprise. She stared at her husband as he moved laboriously to the table and dropped heavily into his seat. His clothing was filthy, and she could smell the alcohol on him from across the room. Her hand trembled at her throat and fear nearly overcame her at the thought of asking the questions she knew had to be voiced.

"Ian, where have you been? You left without a word and you were gone so long that I began to worry."

He didn't answer, but just looked at her through blood-shot eyes.

"A man by the name of Paul Cameron is here, staying in town. He says Abby's missing and he's here to find her. Ian, do you know where Abby is?" Her voice broke on the last words.

For a moment there was silence in the room.

"Taking her didn't work you know. Nothing is going to bring him back." The words were slurred, and Mrs. Finlayson's heart quickened in fear.

"Ian! What have you done? Where is she?"

Mrs. Finlayson's breath caught in her throat when he answered, and in the next instant she was running for the barn.

In record time she had their horse hitched to the wagon and had climbed into the seat. She had just slapped the reins on the horse's back when Paul rode into the yard.

"Follow me!" she shouted to him as the surprised animal broke into a run and headed across the field.

— ❖ —

"Abby, Abby." There were strong hands touching her face, and Abby turned into their warmth. She opened her eyes to see Paul's face swimming above hers, and in the next instant his hands were gently slapping her cheeks and a voice was ordering firmly.

"Don't go out on me, Red. Come on—stay with me. We've got to get you out of here."

"What's wrong?"

"You nearly fainted."

"I never faint."

"We'll argue that another time."

"You're really here? I didn't dream you?"

"I'm here alright, and I'm going to get you out of there."

Watching Paul move away, Abby nearly called out to him in alarm, thinking he was leaving her. But he was right back with a large rock and, after telling her to back away, he began beating on the lock. Abby used the last vestige of her strength to walk out of that shed when the door was open. It was her pride that kept her on her feet. She hated for Paul to see her like this.

He reached for her immediately. "I'm all wet," she protested weakly, and frantically clung to him.

"I don't care" were the words spoken into her hair.

"I prayed you would come."

"And I'm here."

They held one another close before Paul began to lead Abby to the wagon. It was then she saw her mother-in-law. She wanted to call a greeting to her, but everything was growing fuzzy again and the wagon looked a little farther away than it had a second ago. She felt Paul's arms around her and found herself being lifted into the wagon. She was vaguely aware of Paul tying his horse to the back and getting in beside her.

"Where are we going?" Abby's teeth chattered as the wagon lurched forward.

"Back to the house."

"Will Ian be there?" Abby began to struggle in her near panic, but Paul held her tightly.

"Abby, I'm not going to let anything happen to you. But

your dress is soaked and your skin is burning up. We need to get you back to the house."

"I'm not sick."

"Of course you're not," he agreed with her as the wagon dropped into a rut, thinking he would say anything to see her safely back to the house.

She relaxed against him suddenly, and Paul worried that she might have fainted. Her face was so pale against his shirt, her lips bluish from the cold.

"Please, Lord," his heart pleaded, "don't take her away from me."

46

"I kept my promise, Ian."

"It's all your fault he's dead. I wish you were dead, too."

"No, that's not true. I have to stay here and keep my promise."

"It's so hot in here."

"No one will ever find me."

"Oh, Ian, I've fallen in love with Paul."

"How dare he call me Red. Oh, but I love his voice."

"Corrine was so slim. He won't want to touch me."

For two days Abby tossed on her bed and cried out in feverish delirium. Mrs. Finlayson never left her side, bathing her fever as best she could. Paul was on hand and helped any way he could.

As Paul listened to her ranting, his mind returned again and again to the way she had cared for him: her tenderness, her professionalism, even her demands. When she had first come to him, she hadn't even known him, but still gave of herself to see him up on his feet again. Shame engulfed him as he thought of the way he had treated her. He apologized to her even as she slept, hoping that somewhere in her mind she could hear and understand him.

Paul petitioned God constantly that she would open her eyes in recognition of her surroundings. He had something to tell her, and all he could do was pray that she would not reject him.

Abby's sleep was deep at the moment, but her skin was finally cool and had been for several hours. Mrs. Finlayson was taking a nap. Paul sat at the kitchen table trying to stay awake long enough to eat his eggs.

So much had happened in such a short time. But even as emotional and physical exhaustion were crowding in on him, his mind went back to when he arrived in town.

Paul had taken a room at the hotel, sure that Abby was somewhere in Bruce Mines. He had gotten directions to the farm and talked with Mrs. Finlayson after settling in, explaining who he was and about the last time he'd seen Abby. He closed his eyes in a prayer of thanksgiving that he had decided to visit Mrs. Finlayson the very morning Ian came home. Paul had never actually seen the man—by the time they had arrived back at the house with Abby, he was gone—but she was safe, and for now that was all that mattered.

Paul moved to the door a minute later when someone knocked. He stepped quickly aside for the woman on the stoop to enter. It was Abby's mother—he would have known her anywhere.

He saw instantly where Abby got her small frame and full figure and, even though her hair was brown, the eyes regarding him with open curiosity were just as gray as another pair he loved so well.

"I'm Paul Cameron. You must be Abby's mother."

"Yes, I am. She is here, isn't she?"

"Upstairs."

He watched her eyes move anxiously to the doorway leading to the stairs.

"She's sleeping right now, but she's going to be fine."

"I think," she said slowly, taking deep breaths to steady her voice, "I want you to tell me all you can before I see her. You are the Paul Cameron who was in her care?"

Paul assured her of that fact and, after they were seated, he began his story. She was so like Abby in her expressions, and every one of them showed on her face. He could see he had exhausted her by the end of the story, and her eyes were filled with tears upon hearing her daughter had been locked in a shed and then so ill.

"And you're here because you care for Abigail?"

Paul regarded her in silence and then admitted quietly, "I'm in love with her."

The news didn't seem to surprise Abby's mother at all, and she asked simply, "Does Abby know?"

"Yes, she knows. But I'm not sure she believes me." At the confused look that came over Mrs. Pearson's face, Paul went on. "You see, when we first met, I wasn't at all kind to her and, well, she's having a hard time accepting that I could be in love with her and find her attractive."

Abby's mother nodded with understanding. "Does she return your love?"

Paul smiled, "Yes, but she doesn't know it."

Mrs. Pearson had no chance to question this cryptic statement because Mrs. Finlayson came into the room then. The women hugged and more tears were shed. Paul stayed quiet and let them have their time.

"Has Pastor Cameron filled you in?"

"Pastor Cameron? None of Abby's letters said you were a pastor."

"I'm afraid Abby wasn't aware of that fact until some time after we'd met." There was pain evident in both Paul's voice and expression, and both women understood without question.

"I think," Elizabeth Pearson spoke as she stood, "that's it's time I see Abby."

— ✦ —

This time the hands touching her face were cool, and they felt wonderful.

"Are you going to wake up and talk to me?"

"Mother!" Abby's eyes flew open in disbelief at the sound of that voice. "I can't believe you're here."

"And I'm glad you still are. They tell me you've been seriously ill."

"I don't remember very much."

The older woman laughed. "Well, at least we're making progress—you didn't deny being sick."

Abby's smile was small. "I want to wash my hair. It feels terrible."

"Oh, please don't do that to me, Abigail! If your father were here, he'd have a fit that you even suggested such a thing. And then he'd turn to me and blame me for your stubborn personality."

"Yes, Elizabeth." Abby was able to perfectly imitate her father's tone when he was being patronizing, and Abby's mother couldn't hold her laughter.

"Oh Ab, we've missed you so much. And I'm so sorry about Ian." Elizabeth Pearson leaned over to hold her daughter.

Almost two hours later Abby was once again sleeping, but she felt clean inside and out. She had cried herself dry and then taken a bath and washed her hair. When she finally crawled back into bed, her sheets were fresh and she was slumbering within seconds of her head hitting the pillow.

Downstairs, Paul was telling Abby's mother what he thought of her being out of bed.

"Don't you think her hair could have waited?"

"'Waited for what?' she would have said to me."

"Well, you could have told her it's too soon to be out of bed—you're her mother."

Liz Pearson's answer to that was a very unladylike snort. "Really, Pastor Cameron! All those weeks with Abby and you think my being her mother would have the slightest influence on her when she's made up her mind?"

Mrs. Pearson chuckled as though thinking of a private joke, but when she spoke her voice was very tender.

"I don't know if you and Abby are supposed to have a life together. But I can tell you what her father has said about her from the time she was small: 'Living with Abby may be a lot of things, but boring isn't one of them.'"

47

The day was drawing to a close, and Paul sat with the Misses Finlayson and Pearson at the kitchen table. He was headed to see Abby, but for some reason he hesitated.

"So you talked to Ian?" Paul heard Liz ask.

"Yes, at the jail."

"It must be awful for you."

"I knew he was upset, but I never had a hint in all his crazy behavior and then disappearing as to what he was up to. I somehow thought with Abby out of the area he would just try to get over Ian's death like I was. I would never have dreamed he was capable of such a thing."

The table was silent for a moment, and then Mrs. Finlayson spoke to Paul. "I expect you'll want to press charges, Paul, and I don't blame you one bit. Abby's testimony could probably keep him locked up for a long time."

"I'm sure you're right, but you know Abby well and I think you'll agree with me that she probably wants no such thing. I'm sure she just wants to be left alone."

"I think she will be, even if he's let out of jail. I told him I was ashamed of the way he acted, and he cried like a baby." A tear rolled down the grieving woman's face as she went on. "I think he scared himself—he must have. He told me to tell Abby he was sorry."

Elizabeth Pearson reached out and hugged the crying woman. She had been a kind mother-in-law to Abby, and Liz hated to see her suffer so, but she wasn't sorry that Ian had turned himself in to the sheriff. He needed to be locked up—maybe not forever, but he had committed a serious crime that could have cost Abigail her life, and for that he must stand responsible.

"Mrs. Finlayson, I'm confident the sheriff can handle everything without any input from Abby or me," Paul spoke quietly as her tears began to abate. "And right now it doesn't seem like it, but it will be for everyone's good. I trust God—and I know you do also—to take care of all our needs. Even though your husband will have to pay for his deeds, it can still be a time of resting in God's care, a time of renewal and beginnings."

Both women looked at this young man with new understanding as he spoke the words so gently and with such wisdom. The future seemed a little brighter with a glimpse of what a fine pastor this man must be.

Paul smiled at both of them and said they could talk more later, but right now he was headed upstairs. He exited the room hoping to start some beginnings of his own.

The lamp on the table near the bed was turned high, and Abby was reading. She called "Come in" when she heard the knock and waited for the door to open. Paul stood a moment, filling the frame and letting the door swing wide. Both Abby and Paul could hear the women's voices in the kitchen.

Abby hadn't seen him since the day he found her in the shed, or at least she hadn't remembered seeing him. Even though he was in the shadows, she thought he looked wonderful.

Paul was speechless as he gazed at Abby sitting back against the pillows with her hair spread down around her shoulders. All of the words he had rehearsed flew out of his head, and he could only stare. He cleared his throat a few times before anything would come out.

"Abby, can I talk with you a moment?"

"Certainly," she answered without hesitation. "Just give me a moment."

Paul stood in the hallway outside the once-again closed door and rubbed his sweating palms on his pants. He spun quickly when the door opened to find Abby standing there, swathed in quilts.

"Are you sure you should be out of bed?"

"I'm sure. I thought we could talk in the living room."

"Will you be warm enough?"

"I'll be fine. It's probably warmer downstairs than up here."

The descent on the stairway was made in silence. Once in the living room Abby sat quietly on the sofa, while Paul lit the lamps. The room was simply furnished, and Paul thought all the chairs were too far away from Abby, so he sat on the sofa right next to her.

When a few moments of silence passed and Paul had done nothing but stare at her, Abby began to feel self-conscious.

"I think I'm still adjusting to the fact that you're alive. You were so sick and well, when Corrine—"

Abby reached for his hand, and Paul held hers like a man grasping a lifeline. Again there was silence between them and then Paul began to examine the small hand within his own. He lightly traced her fingers before covering the hand with both of his own and holding it tight.

"I don't know if I had the right, Abby, but I asked God to spare you. It was different this time somehow. I mean, I just really knew—that is, after I prayed—that it wasn't God's time for you to go home. But I have to be honest with you, Abby. I asked for a selfish reason: I wanted you for myself. I asked God to spare you so you could be my wife, to go back to Bayfield with me and be at my side in the church there."

They looked at one another in silence, not even hearing the voices in the next room.

"Do you remember what I said to you, Abby, when we were still at Templetons? Well, nothing has changed. I still think God wants us to be together and that we could love each other very much."

"I think so, too."

The words were spoken so quietly that Paul was not sure he'd really heard right. He leaned closer to the woman he loved, his heart thundering in his ears. He had to be sure. "Abby, will you marry me?"

"Yes."

She whispered the word without hesitation, and in the next moment Paul's lips covered her own. The kiss deepened and they held each other close.

"Oh Red, please tell me we can be married right away." Paul spoke finally, his eyes drilling into those of the woman in his arms.

"We can be married right away, but—"

"But what?" Paul felt a sinking sense of dread.

"I want us to be married in Baxter."

Paul's surprise and relief was so great that for an instant he didn't move or speak, and then a huge smile broke across his face and he pulled Abby even closer.

"Why do you want to be married in Baxter?"

"I've already been married in my home church, and your family wants to see you so badly and they missed your wedding with Corrine. We've both been far away from everyone for what feels like a long time, and I think Baxter is the perfect place for our beginning."

"Have I mentioned, Abigail *almost* Cameron, that I'm very much in love with you?"

"Yes, I believe you did say something to that effect. Did I tell you that I love you?"

"No, I don't believe you did." Paul tried to sound casual, not wanting to rush her, but needing desperately to hear the words.

"I love you, Paul."

"When did that happen?"

"In the shed."

"Ahh, Red."

"Shh," she touched his face when his eyes filled with pain. "I won't say it was fun, but I felt God's presence and I also realized how much I need you. It wasn't until I looked up through the bars on that silly door and felt your hands on my face that my heart melted and I knew I was in love.

"I don't remember much after that. Just waking up in the bedroom upstairs and wanting instantly to see you and tell you I love you."

"Say it again."

"I love you."

It was in Abby's heart to say it over and over, but Paul's lips were covering her own again and Abby believed with all of her heart she would have a lifetime in which to tell him.

48

Paul paced around the room and then threw himself onto the sofa in Luke and Christine's living room. He sat still for only a moment before jumping to his feet and bellowing down the hall.

"Luke, you're going to make me late for my wedding, and Abby will be furious!"

Luke stuck his head out of his bedroom door, and Paul could see he didn't even have a shirt on. Paul threw up his hands in frustration. Silas, dressed and ready to go, observed the whole thing dispassionately from a nearby chair.

"I should have ridden in with the girls," Paul grumbled as he began to pace again. Christine, Amy, Joshua, and baby Kate had all gone in early to help Grandma Em, Julia, Susanne, and Abby's mother with the preparations.

"You'd have only been in the way. Not to mention, women have this thing about not being seen before the wedding— tradition and all that. Sit down, Paul. We have plenty of time." Even as Silas spoke the words, he praised God that his wedding was over and Amy was already his.

Paul did sit but was out of his seat the second he heard Luke's steps in the hall. He hustled his brothers out to the waiting wagon as though going to a fire.

Silas drove with Paul next to him, and Luke sat on the backseat. The day was beautiful, and Paul prayed for a calm spirit as they moved toward town. This was a day he wanted to remember forever, and he knew if he continued on as he was, the day would be over before he knew it and he wouldn't know where half of it had gone.

"I apologize if I was rude at the house," Paul said with quiet sincerity to his brothers. To his surprise they both laughed.

"You know, Paul," Silas spoke, "I'd forgotten you weren't at our weddings. Believe me, Luke's actions that day make yours look calm."

"Me?" Luke said with feigned outrage. "Silas, it was you that was so nervous you forgot to keep your place by the pastor. I tell you, Paul, he would have gone up the stairs the moment Amy started down if I hadn't grabbed his arm."

"Well, who could blame me? You should have seen Amy, Paul, standing on the wide stairway at her aunt and uncle's and in that white dress. I fell in love with her all over again in that instant."

"You sound like a newlywed," Luke commented.

"You're not exactly an old married man yourself. As I recall, Christine looked rather nice on your wedding day, too."

"Nice! She took my breath away."

"You sound like a newlywed," Silas mimicked, and the men laughed. Paul was feeling better by the minute as he listened to his brothers' light banter. The wagon was now at the edge of town. As soon as the ceremony started and he could see Abby, all would be fine.

Abby, upstairs at Grandma Em's, was thinking the same thing. She wished there was no tradition about not seeing the groom before the ceremony. She wasn't having doubts or feeling nervous, she just wanted to be married and with Paul.

Was it just three weeks ago they had been sitting in her in-laws living room and she had asked Paul if they could go all the way to Baxter to be married?

The extra days they had spent in Bruce Mines to get Abby back on her feet had been no strain. Even the stop-off in

Bayfield to tell the congregation of their plans had been great fun. But once in Baxter, sewing and planning for the big day, things had gotten a little rough.

Abby and her mother were staying with Grandma Em. Elizabeth had traveled down with Paul and Abby after receiving a wire that Abby's father would be unable to get away from Michigan. He'd sent his love to all. Paul was out at the ranch with Luke and Christine, and Abby keenly felt the separation. Why, they had been together almost constantly for weeks, and each evening when Paul came in to see Abby, it had been nearly unbearable to have him leave again. She wished now that they had gone ahead and married up north and had just planned a reception in Baxter.

"How are things coming, dear?" The door opened and Liz Pearson stepped in, followed by Grandma Em.

"I think I'm all set. I just wish it were all over—the wedding I mean."

The older women both laughed.

"I'll bet you do," Grandma Em said as she hugged Abby. "And if I know Paul, he probably shares your feelings exactly."

"Actually, we came up because Mac is looking for you. He says it's time to leave for the church."

Abby was a vision in cream-colored satin nearly 30 minutes later, as she stood with her hand tucked into the curve of Mac's arm. He had come to her after they had arrived in Baxter and asked for the honor of giving her away.

Abby, desperately missing her father, had hugged him for his sensitivity. She had told him the honor was all hers, and now they stood, so contrasted in size, waiting to walk down the aisle.

The chords on the piano sounded their cue, and they stepped forward in unison. Every eye in the room was on Abby, but she didn't notice. Her eyes were locked with those of a tall man at the front of the church, and she didn't even know when Mac released her.

The ceremony was lovely. Silas played the piano and Amy sang a solo—a wonderful song of commitment and love within God's care. Abby felt as though her heart would burst when Paul looked into her eyes and not at her hand as he placed a simple gold band upon her finger. All the words he'd spoken grew just a bit dim compared to the promise of love she read in his eyes.

The atmosphere of the church had been hushed and reverent throughout the ceremony until the end when Paul kissed Abby briefly, only to snatch her back in his arms a moment later and kiss her again. The room broke up with laughter and put everyone in high spirits for the reception to be held at Mark and Susanne's.

"You can scoop Abby up and leave any time you want." It was several hours later, and the words were spoken by Grandma Em, her eyes twinkling.

"Thanks, Gram," he said as he hugged her. "I think she believes it her duty to see that everyone is happy and comfortable."

"That's what makes her a good pastor's wife. But I'm sure you'd agree—today belongs to the two of you."

They stood for a moment watching Abby with two of her Cameron nieces: baby Kate on her shoulder and Elizabeth in her lap. She looked jubilant as her eyes caught Paul's.

"You need some of your own, Paul," his grandmother whispered quietly.

"I couldn't agree more." His smile nearly stretched off his face as he started for his wife.

Abby did feel a little strange about leaving ahead of the others, but Paul had her out the door and on the way to the hotel before she had too much time to protest.

"We're going to be here for a few days, and I think we'll have time to visit with everyone."

"Oh but I was thinking of you, Paul. It's been so long since you visited with them that I didn't want to rush you away."

"I appreciate that, my love, but like I said, we can see them later." He finished speaking just as they stepped into the hotel and, with the room key in Paul's pocket, started right up the stairs.

All was quiet in the hallway outside of their room, and Paul opened the door before lifting Abby into his arms. The door shut with the help of his foot, and he moved to the nightstand where the lantern stood. Abby struck the match and lit the lamp all from the position of his embrace.

"You could put me down, you know."

"I don't want to put you down."

Abby laughed. She thought he sounded like a little boy whose older brother was trying to take away his birthday present.

The room was bathed with a soft glow from the lantern when Paul sat in the overstuffed chair with Abby in his lap. She snuggled against him thinking how small and protected he made her feel.

"I love you, Red."

Abby's face was radiant as she tipped her head back to stare up at him.

"You," she teased him, "may call me Mrs. Cameron."

Paul's laughter bounced off the walls before he looked into her eyes—eyes filled with love and mirroring his own, eyes that assured him that the long, long road to finding each other had been worth every single step.

Epilogue

Steam blew and doors were opened as the train rumbled to a stop. Mr. and Mrs. Paul Cameron disembarked, shifting packages and bundles as they made their way to the street.

They headed straight for Grandma Em's with one stop for more shifting of the packages.

"Do you think she'll be surprised?"

"I'm not so sure. We write so often, and she knows us pretty well."

"I just couldn't stand the thought of her coming all the way to us, Paul. And it's simply not the same to put it in a letter. But I don't want to upset her."

"I know what you mean, Red, but she'll be worried about you nonetheless."

A few minutes later they stood before the front door. Abby knocked with Paul towering behind her holding the two smallest bundles.

Grandma Em opened the door and gasped, her hands flying to her breast in surprise. Abby immediately stepped forward, hugged her and led her to the couch. Paul pushed the door shut with his foot as he followed.

Grandma Em had still not said a word but watched as Paul moved next to Abby and placed his bundles in his grandmother's arms.

"The one on your right is Jessica Marion and on the left is Julie Marie."

Tears filled the old woman's eyes as she looked in wonder at the infant girls in her arms.

Abby spoke then. "We hope you're not upset, but we just had to come and see you. It's been so long, and this was too special for a letter."

Grandma Em finally found her voice. "But Abby, are you sure you should even be out of bed. Why, these babies can only be . . ."

"Three weeks old, and I'm fine. My date was off and we thought they were early, but the doctor said they're full term."

"None of your letters said it was twins," the older woman accused her grandson with a stern look.

"We didn't know, Gram—not until Jessica was delivered and the pains continued so Julie could arrive."

"Did you have a rough time of it, Abby?"

Paul answered for his wife. "She was wonderful, Gram. The whole thing was over in just a few hours. I wouldn't have missed it for the world."

"You were there, Paul?"

"You bet. The doctor tried to throw me out, but I pulled rank on him and told him God wanted me there, and he gave up."

Grandma Em laughed in delight at this, but the tears were just under the surface and Paul and Abby took their daughters so she could wipe her face. When she had dried her nose, she moved two chairs close to the front of the sofa and Paul and Abby sat. Grandma Em took the couch, everyone's knees nearly touching, and studied her great-granddaughters in their parents' arms.

Her wrinkled, weathered hands reached out to stroke the downy red fuzz on the tops of their heads, and she watched as one baby found her tiny fist and began to suck on it. No one moved from their position until the girls began to fuss from hunger.

Makeshift cribs were made for the babies while Abby fed them in the bedroom upstairs. Paul and Abby put them to bed before rejoining Grandma Em back in the living room.

In a movement as natural as breathing, Paul pulled Abby close the minute they sat down on the sofa. Grandma Em regarded the two of them and then spoke softly. "It's so good to have you here."

"It's good to be here," Abby smiled and answered for all of them.

Paul kissed the top of his wife's head, and then spoke across the room to the woman who had stayed faithful and near him in her prayers, all the years of his life. He knew she would understand his words.

"I chose a rough road, Gram, but Abby was waiting at the end of it. Every time I look at her, I know how much God truly loves me."

About the Author

Lori Wick is one of the most versatile Christian fiction writers on the market today. From pioneer fiction to a series set in Victorian England to contemporary writing, Lori's books (over 1 million copies in print) are perennial favorites with readers. The Place Called Home series is a heartwarming saga of faith and love in the farmlands of Wisconsin.

Born and raised in Santa Rosa, California, Lori met her husband, Bob, while in Bible college. They and their three children, Timothy, Matthew, and Abigail, make their home in Wisconsin.

Other Books
by Lori Wick

A PLACE CALLED HOME SERIES
A Place Called Home
A Song for Silas
The Long Road Home
A Gathering of Memories

THE CALIFORNIANS
Whatever Tomorrow Brings
As Time Goes By
Sean Donovan
Donovan's Daughter

THE KENSINGTON CHRONICLES
The Hawk and the Jewel
Wings of the Morning
Who Brings Forth the Wind
The Knight and the Dove

ROCKY MOUNTAIN MEMORIES
Where the Wild Rose Blooms
Whispers of Moonlight
To Know Her by Name